Mel trembled. She gave a soft
moving with unconscious sensuality, straining against
Crys's body.

Suddenly Crys stiffened and pulled back so that she
could look into Mel's eyes. Mel went to draw Crys back
into her arms, but Crys frowned, whimpering softly.

"No, Mel. Please. We shouldn't be . . . we can't . . .
I . . ." And Crys was moving away, putting cold
distance between them.

Mel had a blinding flash of déjà vu. This couldn't
be happening again. "Crys, please. Don't go. I didn't
mean to —"

Crys stopped and turned back to Mel. "I know you
didn't. It was my fault. I shouldn't have —"

"It wasn't anybody's fault," Mel began.

"Perhaps not. Maybe *fault* wasn't exactly the
word." Crys swallowed, and Mel's eyes focused on the
still erratic beating of the pulse at the base of her
throat. "Look, Mel. I don't want to take advantage of
you at the moment. We've been spending a lot of time
together, and you're vulnerable just now. You've
recently broken up with your boyfriend and —"

"You think I'm pining for Terry? Do you think
that's what this is about?" Mel asked, dismay mixed
with angry disbelief.

"Well, it's very emotionally upsetting and —"

"And don't forget the sex," Mel put in bitterly.

"The . . . I . . ." Crys swallowed again. "I didn't
say —"

"But that's what you meant." Mel suspected she
was being unreasonable, but she couldn't seem to stop
herself. "You think I'm missing sex so much I'd take
it anywhere I can get it. Even with a woman?"

LOOKING FOR NAIAD?

Buy our books at
www.naiadpress.com

or call our toll-free number
1-800-533-1973

or by fax (24 hours a day)
1-850-539-9731

Silver Threads

A novel by
Lyn Denison

THE NAIAD PRESS, INC.
1999

Printed in the United States of America on acid-free paper
First Edition

Editor: Lila Empson
Cover designer: Bonnie Liss (Phoenix Graphics)
Typesetter: Sandi Stancil

Library of Congress Cataloging-in-Publication Data

Denison, Lyn, 1947 –
    Silver threads / by Lyn Denison.
        p.   cm.
    ISBN 1-56280-231-3   (alk. paper)
    I. Title.
PR9619.3.D425S5   1999
823'.54—dc21   98-44747
                                                                                    CIP

For Glenda
my Little Treasure

And for my sister, Lana

About the Author

Lyn Denison was a librarian before becoming a full-time writer. Her partner of nearly twelve years is also a librarian, which goes to prove that tidying books is not all that goes on between library shelves. Lyn lives with her partner in a historic inner-city suburb in Brisbane, the capital city of Queensland, Australia's Sunshine State. Apart from writing she loves reading, talking about books, cross-stitching, and modern country music. Occasionally she ventures out line dancing, which even she will admit is not a pretty sight.

CHAPTER ONE

"Crys?"

"Wow! Two calls in one week, Angela. I'm over-whelmed." Crys Hewitt chuckled softly. "What's the drama?"

"Drama?" Angela Wright's low voice sounded just slightly put out. "What makes you think there's a drama?"

"Well . . ." Crys began, and Angela laughed softly.

"It sounds as though I only ring you when something's wrong, and I guess I do, don't I? I don't mean to. It's just that you're always so, well, calming, I guess."

Crys grimaced unconsciously. "You're the only one who thinks so. And apart from that, more happens in your life than in the life of the average middle-aged matron."

"Middle-aged matron? Now that *was* below the belt."

They both laughed.

"I thought that would guarantee a comment," Crys teased.

Angela sighed."I suppose I am middle-aged. Forty-nine. Two grown-up daughters. Two grandchildren. I certainly don't feel that old," Angela said wistfully.

"You don't look it either," Crys said honestly, smiling as she imagined the other woman looking at herself in the hall mirror of her immaculate home over a hundred miles north of Crys's farm. "So, what's the problem?" Crys asked. Angela sighed again.

"It's Melissa."

Crys paused, not noticing that her fingers had tightened slightly on the receiver. "Mel? What's wrong with her?"

"Nothing life threatening," Angela assured her quickly. "Although Mel might think it is right now. She's broken up with Terry."

"Oh," Crys said uneasily. "I guess she's pretty upset about that."

"She is," Angela agreed. "Not that I'm surprised. You know I've always felt he was something of a layabout. Mel was always so secretive about him. And anyone who's so disinterested in family can't be all good. We never got to meet him, you know," she finished ominously. Crys laughed.

2

"Some people just aren't family oriented, Angela."
She paused. "But you said Mel seemed serious about
him, so I suppose she must be taking the breakup
badly. They've been together for a couple of years now,
haven't they?"

"Mmm. About five or six years, I think." Angela
sighed. "All this happened six months ago, and Mel's
only just told me. Now she wants to come home."

"What's wrong with that? You've been trying to
get her back to Brisbane for years. Ah!" Crys stopped
and lightly slapped her hand to the side of her dark
head. "I'd forgotten. Tasmania. You were off to
Tasmania. So what are you going to do about that?
Let Bill go on his own?"

"Oh, Crys, I'm pulled both ways," Angela said
agitatedly. "You know Bill's totally useless on his own.
He's the real absentminded professor. But I also feel I
should be here for Mel. I know she's twenty-eight, but
she's always been naive in a lot of ways."

"Why not get her to go to Tasmania with you and
Bill," Crys suggested. "Bill's job down there is only for
one semester, isn't it?"

"Yes, but Mel's determined she doesn't want to go
down to Tasmania with us. She said she'd be okay,
that she'd just stay at home on her own, but I don't
think she should. She seemed so down."

Crys frowned. "I see your point. Can't Mel stay
with Amber then?"

"I thought about that, but the house Amber and
Adam are renting is far too small for the four of
them, let alone having an extra adult living there. And
they won't be moving into their new house for at least
a month."

"What about Mel's father?"

"Danny's taken Cindy and the boys overseas on holidays. I thought I'd told you about that. I must have forgotten. Anyway, they won't be back for weeks." Angela paused slightly. "But I did come up with an alternative," she continued. "Could Mel come down to you? You said you needed help on the farm. Mel could do that."

Crys stiffened. "Oh, Angela, I don't know. I can't afford to pay much —"

"You wouldn't need to pay Mel," Angela said blithely.

"Don't be silly, Angela. I'd have to pay her. But it would be almost slave labor, which is why I haven't been able to find anyone to take it on."

"I'm sure Mel would welcome the chance. You and Mel always got on so well. But that aside, it would be a change of scene for Mel, and it would keep her occupied, take her mind off Terry."

"What about her work?"

"She can still do that. She can do her illustrating anywhere."

"I don't think that's strictly true," Crys put in dryly. "But apart from that, you know this place isn't exactly the Sheraton. It's pretty basic, hardly what Mel's been used to."

"You have running water, don't you?" Angela laughed.

"Yes, I have running water, as you also know," Crys agreed in mock exasperation. "Have you mentioned this idea to Mel?"

"Not yet. I wanted to check with you first. So is it okay?"

"Mel might not want to do it," Crys began.

4

"Leave that to me," Angela stated confidently. "Just tell me you'll take her in."

"Take her in?" Crys laughed reluctantly. "You make her sound like an orphan."

"I feel like I'm making her one by not being there for her, but, well, you know what Bill's like."

"More trouble than half a dozen kids?"

Angela laughed. "And then some. I sometimes wonder why I bother."

"Well, don't blame me. I tried to get you to see the light." Crys teased lightly, and Angela chuckled.

"Light, schmight. And I still can't see what you see in it. There's no substitute for, well, what men have to offer."

"Ah! Don't you believe it. Give me a good woman anytime. When she runs her fingers —"

Angela groaned. "You know I can't cope with all that, Crys."

"Of course you can. You can cope with anything," Crys said levelly. "That's what I've always admired about you over the years. How many years is it that we've known each other? Twenty?"

"At least. But let's just keep that to ourselves." Angela sobered. "I really do appreciate this, Crys. You're a great friend. You always have been."

"So have you. Well. If Mel agrees to this, and I can't really see her wanting to exchange cosmopolitan Melbourne for country Uki, when are you expecting her home? You and Bill are leaving this weekend, aren't you?"

"Yes. And Mel's already here. She arrived unannounced last night, complete with suitcases, in the middle of a storm and looking like a drowned kitten."

Angela made a clucking noise. "She drove all the way up here on her own. I'm just glad I didn't know she was doing that or I'd have been worried out of my mind. Anyway, I thought she could come down to you tomorrow or Friday."

Crys absently rubbed at the frown between her eyes. "Angela, I don't know about this. Mel's welcome to stay any time, but this isn't exactly the hub of the social whirl. I don't want you pushing her into coming down here if she doesn't want to."

"I wouldn't do that," Angela pouted.

"Oh, no? You are a professional when it comes to organizing everyone, and you know it. Even if you do wear kid gloves to do the shoving."

Angela laughed again. "All right. I get your point. Mel's out at the moment, but what if I get her to ring you tonight and you can see for yourself how she feels about it? No pressure from me."

Crys paused. "All right. I suppose if I talked to Mel myself —"

"Great. Well, we'll ring back tonight after dinner. Bye. And thanks, Crys."

Crys stood motionless for long seconds until she realized the phone was buzzing in her ear and she gently replaced the receiver on its cradle.

"You didn't think I'd mind?" Mel asked incredulously, more than a little annoyed with her mother.

"Well, no." Angela shrugged her shoulders beneath her designer dress. "You know I'll worry about you if I have to leave you here alone."

6

"Mum, I'm a big girl now, pushing twenty-nine," Mel reminded her mother dryly.

"I know. And you're twenty-eight. You'll be wanting to subtract the years soon enough, believe me. But, apart from that, you'll always be my baby."

"Mum!" Mel shook her head.

"Well, you are." Angela sighed. "And I do worry about you. If your father wasn't overseas you could have gone to him. And Amber's place is too small. So then I thought of Crys. You've known her all your life and I thought you might enjoy a short stay in the country."

"But I haven't seen Crys for years." Not since she'd left school and . . . Mel turned and walked over to the fireplace to hide the slight flush that colored her cheeks. "You can't just foist me on her like this."

Angela waved her slender hand dismissively. "I didn't just foist you on her. I rang her and asked her if you could stay for a while. Crys needs help on the farm." Angela shrugged. "It seemed sensible all around."

Mel turned back to face her mother. "Help on the farm? Mum, I don't know the first thing about farming, and I'm not keen on finding out either. Can you see me mucking out stables?"

Angela laughed. "It won't be anything like that. Crys grows things." She frowned. "What does she call it now? Wild food. Things you don't see growing everywhere. Apparently there's a good market for her produce, especially overseas."

"I can't even keep a pot plant alive, you know that. I'll be more of a hindrance to Crys than a help." Mel sighed exasperatedly. "There's no problem with you going away. I told you I can stay here on my own.

7

As soon as the sale of the flat goes through, I'll go back to Melbourne and get another place."

"Are you sure you can trust Terry to be fair over the sale of the flat?" Angela went off at a tangent. "He never sounded very reliable to me. What if he . . . ?"

"We have a mutual friend who's a lawyer. She's handling all that. It will be all right, Mum."

"I hope so." Angela bit her lip. "I know you don't want to hear this right now, Mel, but I think this might all be for the best. I never felt he was the right man for you."

Mel turned away from her mother again and fingered the china paperweight on the mantelpiece. "It's all relative now."

"There's no chance you'll get back together?" Angela asked softly.

Mel shook her head. "No. No chance." She was quiet for a moment before replacing the paperweight on the mantelpiece and turning back to her mother. She ran her hand through her short hair and sighed. "Life has a habit of going on."

"It does that." Angela walked over and gave her younger daughter a hug. "And wounds do heal." Her hand absently rubbed Mel's back.

A small voice inside Mel told her this would be a good time to tell her mother the truth about Terry. They were alone together with no fear of an interruption. Bill, her stepfather, was at work. Mel could tell her mother Terry was a woman, that she, Mel, preferred it that way.

"That's why I thought getting away from it all, going down to Crys's, would be just the thing for you." Her mother continued, "It's such lovely country around Uki. Green valleys. Rolling hills. So restful."

Mel sighed again. "Mum —"

"Why not ring Crys?" Angela suggested in the coaxing tone Mel remembered so well.

In the past it had been almost impossible to refuse her mother when she used that intonation, and Mel felt herself wavering as usual.

"It won't hurt to talk to Crys, will it?" Her mother persisted. "And then if you don't want to go you can stay here. I could ask Amber to come down to keep you company every so often, just to ensure you're not lonely."

Mel rolled her eyes. "Amber doesn't have time to come running down here to play nursemaid to me. She has her husband and kids to look after. She won't thank you for asking her to do that."

"Of course your sister would come if you needed her. She felt the same way I did about Terry. Why, just the other day —"

"Mum. Okay." Mel held up her hands in surrender. "I'll ring Crys."

"I think that would be best. Her number's there on the pad by the phone."

And the moment of truth seemed to pass. Or Mel allowed it to.

Wiping her damp hands on the hand towel, Crys glanced around the kitchen and decided it was tidy enough. She walked through to the living room and sat down in her easy chair.

Picking up a magazine, she leafed through a few pages. This didn't hold her interest, so she tossed the magazine back onto the coffee table. If she sat here she'd begin to think, and for some reason she didn't want to start delving into the past tonight.

With a sigh she reached for the remote control and began flipping through the channels on the television, stopping on the one-day cricket match between Australia and New Zealand. She'd forgotten that was on today, so she settled back to pick up the threads of the match.

The Aussie team was in a firm position but one just never knew with cricket, especially the fifty-over-only one-day games. The match wasn't over until the last ball was bowled.

When the phone rang she literally jumped in her chair. Her hand went unconsciously to her chest where her heart was pounding with fright. She was halfway to the hallway before she realized she was on her feet, yet when she reached the telephone she simply stood there looking at it for long seconds.

Answer it, she ordered herself forcefully. It would probably be Mel. Unaccountably, her mouth was suddenly dry. She admonished herself and, taking a steadying breath, reached for the receiver.

"Crys Hewitt."

Mel dialed the number and waited as the phone made the connection and rang on the other end of the line. For some reason her palms felt sweaty, and she almost jumped when she heard Crys's deep voice.

"Crys Hewitt."

"Ah. Hi, Crys! It's Mel." Mel cleared her throat. "Melissa Jamieson." She cringed, and her fingers worried at the phone cord. What a stupid thing to say. As if Crys didn't know who she was.

"Hello, Mel." Crys's low voice sounded impossibly lower than Mel remembered, and a tingle of long-forgotten awareness rekindled somewhere deep inside her. "Nice to hear from you. It's been a long time. Must be about ten years or so, isn't it?"

"Um. About that." Mel swallowed again. "Since I left for college in Melbourne."

"That's right. Then we always seemed to miss each other when you came home from art school."

"Yes."

"Congratulations on your success with your books," Crys continued. "Your mother told me all about the Children's Picture Book awards you've won. She's very proud of you."

"Thanks. I . . . it was great to win the awards. It sure boosted our finances." When they'd won the first year they'd put a down payment on the flat together. Terry had decided it would be a good investment. And she had been right, Mel acknowledged. Property prices had escalated in the past few months, and they'd do pretty well out of the sale.

"I'm sure it did," Crys was saying, and Mel drew her wandering attention back to the present.

"Mum says you need some help down there."

"Well, I admit that half a dozen strong pairs of hands wouldn't go astray. So I guess one extra pair would be a start. However, the problem is that the farm is still in its infancy and barely pays its way."

"Oh, I wouldn't take any money," Mel put in promptly.

11

"If you work you need to be paid," Crys came back just as quickly.

They both paused for long moments.

"Mum says you grow, well, things," Mel said, and Crys's soft, deep laughter danced over the phone. Mel changed the receiver to her other hand and wiped her damp palm on her jeans, flexing her fingers where they'd been clutching the telephone.

"I'll bet your mother said I grow strange things."

"Oh, no. No, she didn't. She said it was wild food."

"Something like that."

Mel knew by Crys's tone that she was smiling, and Mel's memory tossed up a vivid picture from the past. They were in their backyard. Crys and her mother were stretched out on bright beach towels, side by side, sunbathing. Mel had to admit that Angela and Crys were as different as chalk and cheese.

Mel's mother was fine-boned and slender, her figure and face barely showing the passage of time. She looked years younger than she actually was even then.

It had always been Mel's bugbear that she didn't take after her mother. She, Mel, was more like her father's family. Her sister Amber, older by four years, had been the lucky one to inherit Angela's genes.

Crys Hewitt, on the other hand, was a little shorter than Angela, with broad shoulders and curving hips, her breasts filling the top of her bathing suit. If Mel could have used one word to describe Crys, she would have said *voluptuous*. Crys was all that the word implied. Voluptuous. And darkly sensual.

Mel flushed at her wayward thoughts and drew her

12

attention back to her phone call again. "Mum showed me the article on your farm that was in the local paper. It sounds interesting."

"It is. But it's hard work. And that's what I think we should talk about, Mel." Crys paused for a moment. "I won't expect you to, well, run yourself ragged. I'll leave it up to you how involved . . . that is, how involved with the farm you want to become. As I said, I can't pay you much —"

"And as *I* said, I wouldn't want any money. I could pay for my room and board."

"You won't have to do that. Bed and board is free to friends. And any work you do on the farm I'll pay you for."

"You might want me to pay you when you find out how hopeless I am when it comes to, well, farms and stuff," Mel said, only half jokingly, feeling more than a little apprehensive.

Crys laughed again, and Mel thought she could listen to that laugh for hours. It was so full of . . . Mel couldn't quite find a word to describe it. It was soothing, yet arousing, relaxing but somehow exciting.

"Are you trying to tell me you don't have a green thumb like your mother?"

"That about sums it up."

"No worries. I'll provide the instruction."

"You're going to have your work cut out for you. I warn you now that when it comes to plants I'm hardly an asset. Punnets of seedlings in shops have been known to feign drooping when they see me approaching to discourage me should I even consider buying them. They know they'd have next to no chance of surviving with me."

Crys's laugh turned throaty, and Mel smiled broadly.

"I promise I'll warn the plants."

"And the animals," Mel added.

"There's only the dog and the cats. Oh, and a few cows in the paddock I lease out. But as far as we're concerned the cows are just part of the scenery."

"I'm relieved about that. And cats I can handle, I think. Not sure about the dog though."

"You'll be fine, Mel." Mel heard Crys take a breath. "So when can I expect you, and do you need directions?"

Mel glanced down at the notepad and grimaced when she saw that her mother had just slipped a written page of directions to Crys's farm onto the phone stand. "Mum's given me a mud map. How about Friday?"

"That will be fine. Well, I'll see you then."

"Yes. Thanks, Crys."

Mel set down the phone. Only then did she realize she hadn't been going to go down to Crys's farm.

CHAPTER TWO

For the second time that day Crys realized she was standing holding a buzzing telephone receiver and she gently set it back in place. Unconsciously she leaned against the doorjamb behind her. And she tried to analyze her feelings.

Mel Jamieson was coming to stay. Her mind flashed up images from the past. Mel as a shy ten-year-old riding her bicycle. Mel climbing the huge poinciana tree between Crys's house and the Jamiesons'. Mel as a quiet fourteen-year-old when her parents divorced.

Crys walked back into the living room and crossed to her overfilled bookshelves. She reached for one of her photo albums, turned to sit down, and rested the album unopened on her lap. Taking a deep breath, she opened the book to the first page.

And there they all were. The first photograph, the colors changing slightly with age, was taken at College's Crossing outside Ipswich nearly twenty years ago, just after Crys had moved in next door to the Jamiesons. Crys realized she must have taken the photograph herself as she was the only one not in the group shot.

There was Angela and her husband, Danny. Crys's husband, Paul. And Amber and Mel. They'd been swimming, and the remains of their picnic lunch lay about them.

Angela sat with shoulders back, looking like a model in her brief bikini, long legs folded neatly beneath her. Danny, her husband, was scowling as he always seemed to be from the time Crys met him until he and Angela divorced.

Paul was grinning, striking a pose designed to set off his well-developed physique. Crys studied the face of her former husband, looked at him without emotion. Until recently she hadn't been able to so much as think of him without bitterness rising within her. She'd never forgive him for what he'd done, but . . . Crys sighed. Life just went on, and hatred was so destructive.

Paul Hewitt was certainly handsome, with a mass of curling dark hair and brooding good looks. Yet she was all too aware that the curve of his smiling mouth could droop sulkily or twist cruelly in the space of a heartbeat.

16

Crys knew she wasn't totally blameless in their fiasco of a marriage. She'd married him for all the wrong reasons and had known even before their wedding day that she was making a big mistake. But, at the time, she'd bowed to convention because she'd felt she had nothing left to do.

She sighed again and shifted her gaze to Amber Jamieson, Angela's older daughter, who was a carbon copy of her mother. Amber had paused in the act of tidying up and Crys smiled faintly. That was Amber, always the little homemaker.

Standing behind her sister was a laughing Mel. She must have been about ten or eleven, long and gangly, her dark hair straggling about her face. Mel was four years younger than her sister and obviously took after her father's family, or so Angela always said. Although Crys could see no resemblance to Danny Jamieson in Mel's face. All that aside, Mel was as dark as Amber was fair.

In the photograph Mel held a slice of watermelon, the juice smeared over her face as she grinned at the camera.

Crys turned a few pages, saw the changes that the couple of years made to Mel. Crys knew Angela felt Amber was the beauty of the family, but as far as Crys was concerned Mel was more interesting. And she had always had an inner glow that her older sister lacked.

Two pages stuck together and fell open at a small studio portrait of a grinning baby, and Crys's heart gave the familiar throb of loss. David, her son. The next photo showed Paul holding David when he was about two years old. Paul was all proud father, and Crys felt the familiar momentary urge to lash out at her husband's smiling face. These were the only two photos she had of her son. She swallowed and made herself keep turning the pages.

And there was Mel looking surprisingly grown-up in high school in her formal outfit, her handsome young escort beside her. Young Gary O'Leary who had lived around the corner. He'd hung around the house for weeks trying to get Mel's attention.

Crys grinned wryly. Gary had been persistent, Crys gave him that, while Mel had been far more interested in swimming and in shooting baskets in netball. Much to her mother's disgust. Crys could hear Angela now.

"But it's so unfeminine, Melissa. Heaven only knows why you want to get all hot and flushed rushing about after that silly ball. Men prefer the waft of subtle perfume, not unpleasant perspiration."

"I don't care what men prefer," Mel had said forcefully. "And I don't smell." She'd turned to appeal to Crys. "Do I?"

"Not that I'd noticed," Crys replied and got a quelling look from Mel's mother for her trouble. "And you can hardly say swimming isn't a clean sport," Crys had added, teasing her friend.

"Swimming only gives you broad shoulders," Angela retorted airily.

"It's healthy, and, apart from that," Mel had stated with youthful arrogance, "I like it."

Crys looked again at the tall sixteen-year-old in her deep maroon dress. She knew Mel hadn't wanted to attend the formal dance, but she'd bowed to her mother's pressure. Crys could see Mel now, sitting at her breakfast bar, frowning intensely.

Mel often unburdened herself to Crys, and Crys had tried to encourage the young girl without doing anything to undermine Angela's directions, although sometimes it had been difficult and called on all Crys's powers of diplomacy.

Why did people dance anyway? Mel had asked Crys. It was a pretty silly sort of thing to do, in Mel's opinion. All sweaty palms and trying to keep to the same beat.

Crys had laughed, secretly agreeing, but of course she couldn't say that or Angela would have been livid with her. Or quietly wounded, which would have been worse.

Mel had confided that she wasn't interested in Gary and worried that going with him to the dance was just giving him false hope. Once again Crys had silently agreed with that, too, but she'd known Angela wouldn't thank her for voicing that opinion.

Having a very attractive mother and older sister had been something of a burden for Mel during her teenage years. And Crys could sympathize with the young girl. Crys had thought Mel's disinterest in dating was her personal adolescent rebellion against her mother.

Yet in the end Mel had gone to the dance with Gary, and less than a week later it had all come to a head. And if Angela had known what —

Crys forced those thoughts right back into the forbidden territory from whence they'd come. Now was not the time to rehash those vaguely confusing memories that still had the power to make her feel so ambivalent, as though something had never been totally resolved. She knew she felt a lingering guilt. But it was more than that.

Crys sighed, her fingers absently tracing the line of Mel's young face in the photograph.

"Oh, Mel," she said softly, the sound of her voice startling her.

She closed the album firmly and stood up to replace it on the bookshelf. There was no use delving into the past. She'd had to come to terms with that often enough in her life.

They were all nearly a dozen years down the track. Mel had grown up. She, Crys, had grown older. They had both followed their chosen paths. Life had gone on for both of them, and it would continue to do so for the short time Mel stayed here on the farm. And it would go on after Mel left.

Crys switched off the television and headed for a hot shower and bed.

Mel knew she should be heading back to her car instead of lazing here on the sand. She'd had an invigorating surf, enjoying the cooling water, the exhilaration of the incessant waves at Burleigh Beach. Then she'd renewed her sunscreen and sprawled out on her beach towel on the warm white sand.

As she'd dried off, she'd absently watched the people around her. The families, parents building sand-castles with toddlers, supervising youngsters boogy-boarding on the waves as they washed up on the sand. There were plenty of muscular young men, tanned, with salt-knotted hair matted by the wind and the sea, their surfboards under their arms, some leashed to their ankles. But Mel only gave them a cursory look.

Her gaze was drawn to the women, women of all ages, all shapes and sizes, all coloring and colors, the tanned and the pale skinned. And she wondered idly how many of those women preferred women.

One in ten supposedly, she told herself. And her eyes went from one woman to another as she speculated about which woman was that one in ten, that one woman who was different. The way she, Mel, was.

Mel's eyes narrowed behind her sunglasses as she noticed a tall young woman who was slowly, almost sensually, rubbing suntan oil into her glistening skin. The woman had an incredible figure. She was dark haired and had long shapely legs. Just like Terry.

The now familiar pain twisted in Mel's stomach and she sighed. *Oh, Terry, why did you —* Mel stopped herself asking the questions that had haunted her for months. There were no answers, so it was pointless going over and over it all the time. Terry certainly hadn't been able to make any rational justifi- cation when Mel had asked her to explain. She hadn't been able, or hadn't wanted, to answer any of Mel's questions.

Why wasn't I enough? Why did you leave me? Why did that giggling twenty-year-old appeal to you over me?

Mel rolled over to her stomach, glad of the anonymity of her sunglasses to hide behind to mask her despair. If anything she felt worse now than she had when it had happened six months ago.

After being together for six years, Mel had thought she'd known Terry so well, thought they were the ideal couple their friends had said they were, that they'd each found the perfect partner in business as well as in their private life.

Of course, they'd had a few problems over the years, but not insurmountable ones. Didn't everyone in a committed, monogamous relationship?

There were only two subjects that had really caused them any ongoing tension. One had been Terry's complete disinterest in family, although in the beginning Terry had been greatly amused when Mel's mother thought Terry was a young man.

Terry's family was in Western Australia, a continent away, and that's how she liked it. All Terry ever said was that her parents were elderly and that they wouldn't understand if she came out to them. *Why stir them up unnecessarily?* Terry had dismissed the subject on more than one occasion. And she said she had no interest in meeting Mel's family. Mel had been disappointed, but she hadn't pressured Terry.

Their other ongoing argument, especially in the beginning of their relationship, had concerned Terry's somewhat irrational fear that other people would discover they were lesbians. Terry had often stated that she hated the label, that the fact she preferred to sleep with a woman had nothing to do with anyone but herself.

Who cared anyway? Mel had replied, and Terry had said their young fans' parents would and Mel had laughed. They'd only had one book published at that stage. It wasn't as though they were household names in children's book publishing. But Terry had been totally convinced they would be. And she'd been well on the way to being right, as it turned out. Now that they had not one but two Picture Book of the Year Awards from the Australian Book Council their names were far more well-known.

Terry wrote the stories and Mel did the illustrations in what were now popular children's picture books. Since they'd won the award, their sales had skyrocketed and, last year, when they'd taken the coveted prize for the second year in a row, well, as Terry had said, it was almost like winning a lottery twice over. Financially, they were more than comfortable.

There had been a certain amount of media interest in the two of them with articles about them in weekend newspapers and in a couple of mass-market magazines. They'd even been interviewed on the *Midday Show* on television earlier in the year.

Terry had been as nervous as a kitten about their television appearance since they'd just bought their new flat. That they'd been living together in a small rented flat for four years before that hadn't seemed to bother her. Fortunately, Terry's fears had been as unfounded as Mel had said they would be. The sympathetic interviewer hadn't even touched on the subject of their living arrangements. The emphasis had been on the fact that they were friends who had met at a party and agreed to collaborate to produce a popular product.

Mel's lips twisted. Friends. Mel had thought they'd become just that from the moment they'd met at that party. Good friends. Actually, it had been after they'd become lovers that they'd decided to write the children's books.

Terry wrote the text. Mel drew the pictures. They laughed together. Made love. It had all been so perfect. But apparently Mel had been the only one who thought so.

Now she was alone, and Terry had moved in with a twenty-year-old who was all adoring eyes and nubile body. Just the way Mel had been seven years ago.

Mel paused. What had made her draw a parallel between herself and Terry's new lover? They were physically totally different, but they did have one thing in common. They were both enamored of Terry. Mel certainly had been. Still was, she reminded herself.

She'd fallen for Terry the night they'd met at a party given by one of Mel's art school classmates. Terry had been at the center of an attentive crowd. Nearly six years older than Mel, Terry was tall and slim and extremely fit. Her dark hair was long and curled loosely to her shoulders.

That first night Mel had watched her with longing, wishing she could be so at ease with a crowd around her, wishing she had the confidence that Terry so obviously had. And wishing she could ask Terry to come out with her, for coffee or something. But of course Mel had been far too reserved to do that. She'd tried once and — Mel stopped those disquieting thoughts.

So Mel had endeavored to be at whatever party or sporting event that Terry attended. She'd joined Terry's adoring audience and eventually she'd got up the nerve to talk to her. Of course, Mel had gained the courage from the measured looks Terry had given her and, after that initial contact, Terry began to seek Mel out, too. They'd talk for hours, go for long walks together and, after what seemed to Mel an eternity of fear and yearning, Terry had kissed her.

Mel couldn't have been happier. They were indeed soul mates. She could barely believe her good fortune.

And she could remember the exhilaration knowing Terry felt the same way she did. When Mel had shyly admitted this to Terry, Terry had laughed, confessing she had been involved with women since her early teens.

Although Terry had been experienced herself, Terry had been Mel's first real lover. Mel shifted uneasily on her towel. Not that she hadn't tried to . . .

She swallowed. Her first clumsy attempts at seduction just before she turned seventeen had been such a humiliating failure Mel hadn't had the nerve to try again. She'd forced that part of her life into the dim, dark recesses, never again to see the light of day.

And she hadn't told a soul about it until she had divulged some of it to Terry. To Mel's disappointment, Terry had been highly amused. Occasionally she'd even resorted to teasing Mel about her youthful infatuation, and Mel had told herself she should lighten up about it. It had happened years ago. She'd grown past it. Or she should have. Yet it still had the power to unsettle her.

But, all that aside, if it hadn't been for Terry, perhaps Mel would still be denying her sexual preference. For she'd kept that buried inside her until she met Terry.

When Terry kissed her it was as though all the doors inside her she'd slammed shut had burst open and everything was swept into a whirlwind to settle back into a new and so-right place. Terry had been so intelligent . . . so attractive . . . so passionate.

Mel brought Terry's beautiful face into focus, and her heart ached with loss. And then suddenly Terry's features disappeared and she found another face sharpening in her thoughts. Hair darker than Terry's.

Eyes deep brown where Terry's had been hazel. A full, generous mouth with the hint of a dimple in one cheek.

And she remembered that other, incredible kiss. The terror. The feverish excitement of it. In those few precious moments Mel's whole world had stood still and spun dizzily at one and the same time.

Yet that ill-advised attempt to find herself, to sort out her confusion, had gone so very wrong. Mel grew hot; her insides turned to water. Recalling that day all those years ago still had the power to disturb her, make her feel again her burning mortification. And also embarrassingly titillated.

Now, here she was heading south to visit, to stay with, the very woman who had been the object of her awkward adolescent crush, the woman she'd inexpertly tried to seduce over ten years ago.

CHAPTER THREE

Mel climbed into her maroon BMW and took a last look at the rolling surf and white sand before she turned out onto the highway.

The car had been Terry's idea, although Mel had to admit that the sedan's sleek lines impressed her. Terry didn't care for driving and she preferred to be driven, so she left the ferrying around to Mel.

"We're going places, Mel," Terry had said. "We can't be seen driving around in your old heap. Let's be more flamboyant. We can go halves in the payments."

27

And so they'd traded in Mel's ancient Holden that had seen better days, and after the initial few months Terry had forgotten her part of the commitment and Mel had continued to make the payments on her own.

Luckily, when they broke up Terry had decided Mel may as well keep the BMW. She decided she wouldn't be needing it as her new girlfriend drove a two-seater sports car. And Terry had spoken as though she had been doing Mel a favor. It still rankled with Mel. It wasn't the money so much as the offhand way Terry had treated her.

Mel sighed. No point in rehashing all that. It would only send her into a depression again.

She followed the stream of traffic, which was surprisingly light for a Friday afternoon. Mel glanced at her watch. She'd been wise heading off now. In an hour or so the volume of traffic would peak and she would have been traveling at snail's pace along the coastal road.

She skirted the main Coolangatta business district and crossed the border between Queensland and New South Wales. She was amazed at the changes in the few short years since she'd visited the area. New roads, new bypasses, new businesses sprouted like mushrooms.

Once over Sextons Hill and the Chinderah bridge, the countryside flattened, the road winding through cane fields that stretched toward the low hills to the west and toward the Pacific Ocean to the east. Eventually she picked out the distinctive shape of Mount Warning.

Sugar-cane fields closed in on the road, and soon she was following the wide Tweed River into

Murwillumbah. As she waited at a set of traffic lights, she scanned her mother's directions.

She had to drive through the city and take the left turn to Uki, *pronounced YOU-kye, rhyming with sky,* her mother had reminded her. Mel smiled to herself as she drove through the suburbs and found her turnoff. Then she was back in the open countryside.

On the left were spreading old trees, she-oaks following the creek bed, and grassy paddocks, green from recent rain, and a scattering of healthy-looking cattle grazing contentedly. To her right were the seemingly never-ending fields of sugar cane.

Mel followed the winding narrow roads and admitted that it was certainly picturesque country. As the hills grew closer, she crossed a low wooden bridge, the loose planks rumbling beneath her tires. Passing a farm market stall, she caught a glimpse of red tomatoes and yellow hands of local bananas.

She slowed on a straight stretch of road and looked at her directions again. There was the turnoff to the Mount Warning National Park.

Then she was passing through the small country town of Uki. A few scattered buildings peeped out between trees and shrubs, and there was an old bank building and the ubiquitous pub. According to Mel's mother, Crys's farm wasn't far past the township.

As she left Uki behind she passed a VW camper painted in iridescent purple and decorated with painted yellow daisies. She smiled. She wasn't far from the hippie settlement of Nimbin, made popular in the sixties when it was taken over by the flower people.

Mel sighed. Maybe they had a point. It must be relaxing to get back to nature and out of the rat race of the cities. More power to them, be it flower or the weed. Mel chuckled and then sobered.

She remembered when Terry had coaxed her into having her first joint of marijuana, not believing Mel had never tried it. Mel had felt very naive. Much to Terry's disgust it had all been a pointless operation anyway. Mel had simply fallen asleep. No highs. No lows.

Perhaps Mel had been a bit of a country bumpkin when she'd first gone down to college. Could it only be ten years ago? It felt like eons.

Mel felt a wave of self-pity wash over her. No wonder Terry had found there was something missing from their relationship. Maybe Mel should have been more forceful, more opinionated, more challenging.

She took a deep breath and accelerated, picking up her speed a little. Hadn't she decided wallowing in the past was a waste of time? Bemoaning what might have been certainly wasn't going to change anything. Terry was gone and she, Mel, was on her own. She had to get on with her life.

She rounded a sweeping curve, and there was the blue bridge her mother had marked on the map. If her mother's directions were correct, and Mel conceded Angela's mud maps were famous for their accuracy and detail, the turn onto Crys's property should be just about here. And there it was.

Turning between the open gateposts, she slowly crossed the cattle grid. She drew to a halt and looked up toward the hills. On her left she could see a house behind a stand of trees, but she knew that wasn't Crys's place. She had to continue past that and on up the long driveway.

Mel bit her lip. Butterflies fluttered in the pit of

her stomach as an attack of nervousness took hold at the thought of seeing Crys again. Now that she was here she wished she was still driving along the highway. Or better still, she wished she hadn't allowed her mother to talk her into coming down here at all.

If it hadn't been for that one awful occasion, Mel would have been looking forward to seeing Crys again, for they had been good friends. And it had been Mel who had spoiled that.

Mel supposed that the problem began back then with the school dance. Well, it had been there years earlier in the form of a vague disquiet. But it was around the time of that final school dance when Mel was nearly seventeen that Mel acknowledged to herself that she had a problem.

She guessed it sort of accumulated and then landed on her about then. Her friends had all been in a fever of excitement over their formal school dance. Mel tried to get into the swing of it but failed miserably. She was terrified someone would ask her to go, while at the same time her friends were petrified that no one would ask them.

When Gary O'Leary, who lived around the corner from Mel's place, asked her to be his partner, Mel had stood there frozen, unable to speak. He'd blushed and repeated his invitation, and Mel suddenly heard herself accepting.

Afterward she could only hope she'd imagined the whole thing, but when Gary kept appearing to walk her home she knew that her nightmare was reality.

Amber was away, so she couldn't ask her older sister's advice. The other alternatives were her mother or Crys. Mel had wanted to talk to Crys about it, but for some reason she felt agitated at the very thought of bringing up the subject with the other woman. So that left her mother.

"Why on earth don't you want to go to the dance with Gary?" asked her mother when Mel finally approached her. "Isn't he that rather nice looking boy who was hanging around here a few months ago?"

"I suppose he's okay looking," Mel had agreed.

"O'Leary? I've met his parents at PTA meetings. They're interested in the school, so they can't be a bad family."

"It's not exactly Gary," Mel said carefully. "I'd just really rather not go to the dance at all, Mum," Mel put in. "I don't care for all that stuff."

"Stuff. You know I dislike you using that word, Mel. It makes you seem as though you have no vocabulary. And every girl likes to go dancing. It's part of your, well, social development."

"Social development?" Mel made a face. "Then maybe I'm just a late developer," she said sarcastically, and her mother frowned.

Fortunately they were interrupted at that moment by a knock on the door.

"It's me." Crys Hewitt walked into the kitchen. "I've just made some cookies. Got time for a cuppa?"

Mel hesitated. Should she leave Crys and her mother alone or stay? Would her mother bring up the subject they'd been discussing? Mel hoped not.

"Always time for a cup of tea." Angela took down her teapot and began her tea-making ritual. "Put the kettle on, Mel."

Crys and Mel shared a conspiratorial grin. Crys, much to Angela's disgust, used teabags, and Angela never failed to belabor the point that there was a right and wrong way to make tea. Using teabags was the wrong way.

"How are things?" Angela asked her friend as Crys set down a plate of delicious-looking chocolate chip cookies.

Crys slid a quick glance at Mel before shrugging. "Still the same. So, Mel. How was school?"

Mel knew there was something going on that Crys and her mother didn't want her to know about. And whatever it was had started about two weeks ago. She'd known that Crys's marriage wasn't happy and about the divorce and what came after it. But Mel knew there was something else.

And she felt some resentment that her mother and Crys were keeping secrets from her. Why did they treat her like a child? Did they think she was still a baby? She was almost seventeen. Some girls were married at that age. Not that Mel knew any but, well, they were.

She knew all about Crys's problems, about her being a lesbian. Everyone knew. Who around here wouldn't know after the huge scandal of the trial!

Mel looked across at Crys, tried to imagine her in the arms of another woman, and hurriedly pushed the thought away. It made her feel strange, all hot somehow, as though she was blushing all over.

She realized Crys was looking at her, and Crys raised her dark eyebrows. Mel's flush deepened.

"School? Oh. It was okay," she stammered, and her mother made irritated tsking noises.

"I don't know what we're going to do with this

young woman of ours, Crys," Angela remarked. "A nice young man has asked her to the school dance, and she doesn't want to go."

Crys gave Mel a sympathetic look. "She doesn't have to go with a guy just because he asks her. She has the right of refusal."

"Well, she's accepted," Angela stated, warming the teapot before adding the tea leaves. "And now she wants to change her mind."

"I see," Crys murmured noncommittally.

"I just, well, he took me by surprise, and I wasn't thinking," Mel explained, her look appealing to Crys for assistance.

"So who is this young cavalier who swept you off your feet?" Crys asked.

Mel rolled her eyes. "He wished!" she said forcibly.

"Gary O'Leary," Angela supplied at the same time.

"Ah. That young man who often hangs around here hoping to catch a glimpse of you, Mel?" Crys teased and Mel blushed.

"He doesn't hang around waiting to see me," she denied.

Crys laughed softly and patted Mel's arm. "I'm sorry, Mel."

The feel of Crys's warm fingers, a transitory touch, lingered long after Crys had released Mel's arm.

"It's cruel of me to goad you over a sensitive subject," Crys apologized. "Why don't you want to go to the dance with Gary?"

"She says she doesn't like dancing," Angela exclaimed.

Mel frowned at her mother. "It's not really Gary himself," Mel said slowly and then shrugged. "I don't know. It's just that the whole scene isn't my idea of fun. I hate dressing up and having guys eyeing me up and down as though I'm a prize cow or something."

"I can relate to that," Crys put in dryly. Before Angela could rebuke her, she continued. "Why don't you just tell Gary you've changed your mind and have decided not to go to the dance?"

"Crys!" Angela admonished. "Of course she's going to the dance. All her friends are going. Amber loved the school dances."

Mel grimaced, and Crys bit off a chuckle. "Haven't you been to a school dance before?"

Mel shook her head as her mother set the milk jug and matching sugar bowl on the table beside Crys's cookies.

"She didn't tell us they were having dances," Angela told Crys in exasperation. "I only found out about this one from one of her friends."

Crys stirred a teaspoon of sugar into her tea. "I guess you have to try a dance at some time, Mel. You might find you have a great time."

Mel mumbled disbelievingly and reached for the consolation of one of Crys's famous cookies.

And by the time the evening of the dance rolled around, Mel felt even less like attending. Her mother and sister and Crys were assembled in the living room as they waited for Gary to collect her.

Mel's tummy was queasy, and her mother was driving her crazy tweaking her hair and patting the folds of her dress.

"Leave her alone, Mum," Amber said, giving her younger sister a sympathetic look. "She looks fine."

Crys nodded. "You look wonderful, Mel. That color suits you." She smiled. "Young Gary's eyes are going to pop out of his head when he sees you."

"And I hope they roll across the floor and out the back door and we won't be able to find them and then I won't have to go with him," she finished ghoulishly.

"Melissa! That's disgusting!" exclaimed her mother.

Mel saw Crys hide a grin, and she giggled hysterically. "I'm sure Gary's father wouldn't let him drive his car without his eyeballs."

Amber groaned. "You can be so gross, Mel."

Mel laughed again but quickly sobered when the doorbell pealed.

"I'll get it," said Mel's stepfather as he joined them.

Mel looked desperately at Crys, who stood up and gave her a squeeze.

"You'll be fine," she said softly. Mel wanted to cling to her, hide her hot face against Crys's full bosom.

"I want a good look at this young whipper-snapper," Mel's stepfather was saying

Mel cringed. "Oh, good grief! I'm not going to marry him, for heaven's sake," she stated through gritted teeth.

Amber laughed. "You're safe, Mel. And you'll have to wait. It's a rule that the older daughter has to get married first."

Well, that had gone to plan, Mel reflected with amusement. Her sister had met a very nice young man and married him just after Mel met Terry. Amber and Adam, referred to by Terry as the A-team, were still happily married and had presented Mel's mother with two grandchildren. At least that had taken some of her mother's focus off Mel, for which she was very grateful.

Mel sighed. She wished all her plans had worked

out as well as her sister's had. Then maybe she wouldn't be sitting here nervously contemplating the meeting ahead.

Even though she hadn't seen Crys for years, Mel had known her since she was ten years old. Yet she couldn't imagine how things would be between them after so long. Not after what had happened between them.

Well, she couldn't sit here all afternoon. It was time to find out the answer to that question. Mel took a steadying breath. The time had come, the walrus said. And apart from that, the people in the other house might think she was casing the joint, planning a robbery. Biting off a slightly distraught laugh, Mel accelerated up the driveway.

Crys knew Mel was coming before she heard the car. Rags stood up and bounded to the front of the shed, giving a warning bark.

"Rags. Here, boy," Crys said firmly. The dog reluctantly returned to stand by Crys's side.

She set the pot she was holding back on its stand and removed her gloves. She crossed to the sink and soaped, rinsed, and dried her hands and forearms. Then she found herself unconsciously running her hand over her hair.

Shaking her head, she took a deep breath and walked out to the cemented apron in front of the shed and glanced past the house to the driveway. Crys paused, Rags right beside her, growling softly in his throat.

"It's all right, boy," she said softly, rubbing his

ears before taking hold of his collar. "This is a friend. And unless she's changed a great deal, I think you'll like her."

A maroon BMW navigated the last bend in the narrow driveway and drew to a halt in front of the carport that housed Crys's old VW. Long seconds later a tall figure climbed from the car and straightened before slowly removing her sunglasses.

Crys watched as Mel looked around, pausing as her gaze settled on the older woman and the dog.

Had Mel always been this tall? Crys wondered. Her hair was dark, the sun highlighting the auburn tinge, and it was cut short and spiked, a few strands falling forward onto her brow. She wore tailored denim shorts and a loose blue T-shirt with something emblazoned on the front.

Rags gave a soft bark, and Crys made herself move forward again, her hand indicating to the dog that he follow.

Mel felt the throb of her pulse as she caught sight of Crys. She had a large dog of some indeterminate breed beside her. Mel raised a tentative hand.

"That's not an attack dog, is it?" she asked as Crys strode forward.

"Not unless he's given explicit instructions," she said with a smile as Mel closed the car door. "Welcome to the farm," Crys said easily. "Your mother's famous directions win out once again I see. How are you, Mel?"

Mel gave a quick smile. "Not bad," she replied and looked around her.

Apart from the house there was a huge shed that was enclosed on three sides. Mel could see an old tractor and another piece of machinery she couldn't identify. There was also a small trailer parked off to one side. Crys's old yellow VW, the one she'd had for as long as Mel could remember, was tucked under the carport by the house.

"Thanks for letting me come visit you," she added politely.

Crys chuckled. "You're welcome any time, even if your mother did orchestrate this visit."

"Trying to distract Mum when she's in full stride is as impossible as it always was." Mel shrugged lightly. "It was easier to go with the flow. But Mum was right. It's lovely countryside down here, and it is great to see you again."

Crys inclined her head. "Likewise. So, come on around the front of the house and admire my view."

Mel walked with Crys and the dog along the side of the house and up the few steps to the covered veranda.

Crys's house was set low and constructed of roughly hewn brick, giving it an aura of age. The building was on the crest of the hill, and wide verandas ran around the entire house, taking advantage of its three-hundred-sixty-degree view.

The back afforded a view of rolling hills while the front overlooked a low, wide valley with a tree-lined river at the bottom that rose to rolling hills again. Through a break in one group of trees Mel could see the road she'd just driven along, and there was the blue bridge she'd crossed.

Also through the trees was the roof of the other small house below, closer to the road, the one Mel had passed as she drove up the hill. It was nice to know Crys's house wasn't completely isolated.

"This is a fantastic position," she said, impressed.

"I think so." Crys smiled. "I had this built three years ago when I sold off the other house and some of the land."

"That house down there I can just see through the trees?" Mel asked.

"Yes. You would have passed it on the way up the hill. It was the original house on the property, and we lived there for years. But I felt this was the prime position for the house." She shrugged. "I sold the old house and five acres and lived in the trailer out by the shed while this house was being built."

"You lived in that small trailer I saw? But it's smaller than my first flat."

"I did. For about six months. And it's called *compact*." Crys laughed softly at Mel's expression. "Now where's your adventurous spirit?"

Mel grinned reluctantly. "I guess it could have been fun."

"It was. But, quite frankly, I have to admit I was glad to move in here and spread out again. Come on inside and I'll show you your room."

Mel followed Crys through a pair of French doors and across the polished wood floor of the living room. With Crys leading the way Mel found her gaze drawn to Crys, the back of her dark head, her broad shoulders, narrow waist, and the fullness of her hips in her faded jeans.

Mel swallowed and made herself look around the room at the comfortable-looking lounge arranged around the brick fireplace. Bright scatter rugs made the room seem homey and welcoming.

"This is the living room. Obviously." Crys gave Mel a quick smile over her shoulder as she opened the door that led into a wide hallway.

"The house has three bedrooms, but I use one as a study." She indicated a small room on her left. "It has good natural light so if you like you can use it if you want to do some of your own work. My room's at the end there, and this is yours. The bathroom's across the hall next to the study."

The room Crys showed Mel into was light and airy and held a double bed covered by a bright crocheted spread in a rainbow of colors. A small chest of drawers was on one side of the bed, and Crys crossed the room to slide open a large, built-in cupboard.

"Hanging space here and drawers over there," she said easily.

Mel walked over to the French doors that opened out onto the veranda. "Here's that wonderful view again." She turned. "Wow! You can lie in bed and watch the sun come up over the mountains. Is the view exclusively for visitors, or do you have the same outlook from your room, too?"

"Yes, I have it too. I designed the house specifically to take advantage of the views. We have some impressive sunsets sometimes."

"It's a great place, Crys," Mel said sincerely.

"Thanks." Crys smiled and glanced at her wristwatch. "Well, I was planning on having dinner in about an hour. How does that sound?"

"I'm ready whenever you are." Mel swallowed and continued quickly. "I'll just go out to the car and get my stuff. I stopped off for a surf at Burleigh on the way down and I'm all salty, so maybe I've got time for a quick shower."

"Sure. I'll give you a hand with your bags."

"One bag." Mel held up her finger. "Oh, and my drawing case. I'm traveling light."

Crys laughed, and Mel followed her out to the car. Rags had raced around the house and bounded up to Mel as she walked outside. She paused gingerly, but he only sniffed her interestedly.

"He doesn't bite," Crys assured her. "At least, not invited guests."

Mel extended her hand slowly, and Rags sat down while she rubbed his ears.

"If he was a cat he'd be purring." Crys smiled at the dog. "You old softie, Rags." She looked back at Mel. "Now, if you like you can put your car in the shed over there. There's plenty of room and it will be under cover," she suggested. Mel opened the door and slid behind the wheel.

Rags stood up and gave a whine, almost as though he was begging Mel not to leave.

"Looks like you've won a heart," Crys said lightly.

Mel made a face. "That's me, a real Pied Piper when it comes to dogs and kids."

"Not a bad representation. They say if dogs and kids like you, you can't be all bad."

Mel twirled an imaginary mustache and started the car.

Crys followed her up to the shed, the dog tagging along, and she showed Mel where to park the BMW.

"Nice car," she said, "and beautiful finish." She ran her hand over the maroon duco as Mel climbed out.

"Well, it's eye-catching," Mel agreed as she opened the trunk. "Actually, I was thinking I might sell it and get something a little less ostentatious."

"That would be a shame." Crys sighed. "I've always wanted a car like this."

"You have?" Mel raised her eyebrows. "Well, it just so happens I know where you can get one." She grinned and pointed to the BMW. "One careful owner, a woman loved by dogs and kids, who only drove it to church on Sundays."

Crys laughed. "I wish I could afford it."

Mel swung her bag out of the trunk and put it down on the floor. "Next best thing. You can drive it while I'm here."

"That's very generous of you."

"Oh, I think I can trust you."

There was suddenly an imperceptible tension in the air between them, and Mel turned back to the car and collected her drawing case. Crys stepped forward and picked up Mel's bag. Mel started to protest.

"It's okay. I can manage one small bag," Crys told her. "And you were right, you do travel light."

Mel locked the car and they walked back toward the house. Dusk was settling over the valley, and deepening shadows added a new dimension to the view.

Mel slid a sideways glance at the other woman as they walked along. Crys stopped every so often to toss a stick for the dog, who came panting back with it.

Crys looked . . . looked what? Mel asked herself. Healthy. Wholesome. Vibrant. She barely seemed any older than the Crys Mel remembered from her adolescence. Her dark hair was a little shorter and perhaps there were a few flecks of gray showing at her temples, but it was as though the years between had never been.

And Mel was shocked at how familiar the other

woman was to her. She remembered the soft curve of her cheek, the nose Crys had always thought was too small for her face, her dark eyes fringed by long lashes, and her full, almost sensual mouth.

Mel shivered and stumbled, making herself concentrate on the pathway back to the house. Of course she would remember Crys well, she reassured herself. Hadn't she known her since she was a child?

Oh, yes, jibed an inner voice. *You've only been here ten minutes and you're allowing yourself to feel, to think inappropriate thoughts about the other woman. Not the best of starts, Mel,* she chastised herself as she followed Crys inside.

"I've put some fresh towels in the bathroom," Crys was saying easily as she set Mel's bag in Mel's room. "Just let me know if there's anything else you need. I'll go see to dinner."

Mel thanked her, and Crys left. On her own again, Mel let the breath she seemed to have been holding escape from her lungs. Well, they'd got over their first meeting and everything seemed to be going reasonably okay, she decided. Perhaps it wouldn't be as awkward as Mel had imagined it would be.

She dug into her bag for fresh underclothes, clean jeans, and a light sweater. Since the sun had slipped behind the hills, Mel could feel the air grow cooler.

In the bathroom she peeled off her clothes and stepped into the shower recess. The warm spray felt divine, and she began to soap her body, washing off the salty residue left by the ocean.

Crys had set out a couple of different cakes of soap, and Mel had chosen what looked like a block of natural soap that had a faint scent of vanilla.

"Just let me know if there's anything else you

need," Crys had said. Mel sighed. Crys had provided everything. Towels. Shampoo. Soaps.

Mel paused as she ran the foaming soap over her breast, her stomach, and she shivered again. Suddenly she imagined Crys joining her in the shower cubicle, her body moving slowly closer until her naked breasts, her stomach, her thighs, pressed against Mel's. And she felt a long-dormant stirring between her legs.

Mel moaned softly. What was wrong with her? She didn't usually go in for such vivid fantasizing.

And in the months since Terry had left her, Mel had felt as though all her senses, her feelings, had frozen. Oh, she'd been going through the motions of living, existing on a superficial level. But deep down, way inside her, she'd felt as though she'd ceased to feel anything. Even thinking of Terry and their love-making had left Mel vaguely dissociated.

Now here she was suddenly all hot and bothered about Crys Hewitt. And Crys's body.

It was the warm water when she was feeling cool, she told herself, and began to vigorously wash herself, adding some cold water to the shower to rinse off the suds. Cold water to douse her hot thoughts.

She grimaced. Crys certainly still had all the feminine curves in the right places, and she moved with a lithe, sensual grace that Mel didn't know she'd remembered until she'd seen the other woman again.

Closing her eyes, Mel let the water cascade over her. What would Crys say if Mel admitted her fantasies? She'd tell Mel to pack her bag and leave, that's what she'd say, Mel told herself.

She determinedly climbed out of the shower, dried herself, and quickly donned her clothes before rubbing her damp hair with her towel. She ran a quick comb through her spiky cut and wiped the condensation from the mirror to peer critically at herself.

She was too thin in the face, giving her a lean and hungry look. She knew she hadn't been eating properly lately, but cooking for one seemed too much of an effort. And there were faint dark circles under her blue eyes. Crys would be hard pressed not to notice the difference in Mel. She was a long way from the dewy-eyed, flush-cheeked teenager who had had a burning crush on the other woman.

And yet, not so far removed. Her reaction to seeing Crys had dredged up all those old longings. The urge to hold Crys in her arms again seemed as strong now as it had been all those years ago. And Crys was still as beautiful, as desirable, as she had been way back then.

Mel rubbed an agitated hand over her eyes. What sort of person did all this make her? For the past six months she'd been nursing a broken heart over Terry's duplicity, and now she was lusting after another woman.

What should she do? Maybe it was just a passing thing, she told herself. Tomorrow it would all fall back to an even keel.

And if it didn't, well, there was only one thing for it, Mel decided. She'd just stay for a few days to satisfy her mother and then she'd go back to Brisbane. The last thing Crys would need was a brokenhearted, lovesick admirer from her past on her hands.

She closed her eyes and leaned her forehead against the cool mirror. She had a sinking feeling it was going to be a long few days.

CHAPTER FOUR

Crys measured out some rice, added twice as much water, and put the bowl in the microwave. While the rice cooked she set two places on the small table in the dining room. The casserole was ready, warming on the stove top.

Would Mel notice that Crys had cooked her favorite, apricot chicken?

Crys paused as she took down two delicate wine-glasses. Well, apricot chicken used to be Mel's favorite, she reflected. Perhaps Mel's tastes had changed in the past ten years. Crys grimaced. You could probably safely bet on that.

Crys sighed. She'd had to cook something. Why not apricot chicken? It was easy and relatively foolproof. The fact that it was Mel's favorite wasn't the only reason she'd chosen to make it. She was simply being a thoughtful host. Wasn't she? Or was she deluding herself?

Taking the bottle of wine from the fridge she set it in the clay cooler on the table. She'd chosen a light white wine from Stanthorpe, hoping Mel would like it as much as she did. Crys stopped again. She didn't even know if Mel drank wine.

In fact, she knew very little about this so very grown-up Mel. Oh, physically she'd changed very little. She was thinner, yet Crys would have known her anywhere. But there was an air of assurance about her now.

Crys shook her head. And why wouldn't there be? The last time Crys had seen Mel she'd been an awkward teenager. Now she was twenty-eight, a successful illustrator, and a confident young woman. Yes, Mel Jamieson had indeed grown up.

And she was very attractive, Crys acknowledged. Angela had once referred to her younger daughter as her ugly duckling, an opinion that Crys had challenged forcefully at the time. Well, Angela's so-called ugly duckling had developed into something of a swan. Crys almost laughed at her flight of fancy.

Yes, Mel *was* an attractive young woman. Her long legs and firm, shapely body—

Crys pulled herself up. Suddenly she felt a throb of tension in the pit of her stomach that was as surprising as it was disturbing. It was a long time since she'd had that particular sensation of awareness, that spiral of sexual wanting.

She walked quickly around the breakfast bar and back into the kitchen, glanced at the rice still turning on the microwave carousel, and crossed to the sink and back again, trying to calm her unexpected rush of agitation.

She had no business even thinking of traveling down that path with this particular woman. It was inappropriate, she told herself vehemently. Totally inappropriate. Mel was Angela's daughter. Angela was her oldest friend, and she had entrusted Mel to Crys's care. Mel needed to be taken care of, not taken advantage of.

Yet knowing all that didn't prevent Crys from having to admit to herself that in another place and time she would have found herself attracted to someone just like Mel. Not just physically but . . . there was something else about Mel. There always had been. And Crys had to curb her recurring inner turmoil.

She'd do well to remember that, apart from anything else, she was fourteen years older than Mel. What would an attractive young woman see in a forty-two-year-old who was fast approaching her use-by date?

Crys exclaimed softly in self-disgust. She was nothing but an old perv, she told herself and wrinkled her nose at her indistinct face reflected in the microwave door.

But there *had* always been some kind of bond between Crys and Mel, even when Mel was a child. They'd always been tuned to the same wavelength, laughed at the same jokes. That bond had remained intact as Mel grew up. When it had undergone an imperceptible change Crys couldn't quite recall, but when Mel had kissed her all those years ago —

The microwave dinged the end of its cooking cycle and Crys pushed those dangerous reminiscences out of her mind. She set about washing the rice until it was light and fluffy.

"That's good timing." Crys smiled as Mel joined her.

"Smells delicious," Mel said lightly and stuck her hands in the pockets of her jeans.

Had she imagined that Crys's dark gaze had moved over her? Mel went hot at the thought. Then she chastised herself, telling herself it was her vivid imagination, a leftover from her sybaritic thoughts while she showered.

Mel glanced at the table, neatly set, and noticed the unopened bottle of wine in the cooler. "Shall I open the wine for you?" she asked. It would give her something to do, keep her thoughts away from other perilous ramblings.

"That would be great." Crys handed Mel the opener, and their fingers touched fleetingly.

Mel felt a surge of sensual awareness, and her body tensed, her heartbeats tripping all over themselves, making her slightly breathless.

"I'll dish up our meal while you're doing that." Crys turned back to the kitchen, and Mel took a steadying breath to regain her composure.

"I was hoping you'd like some wine," Crys was continuing. "I rarely open a bottle when there's just me drinking it. Seems something of a waste to open a whole bottle for one person."

"You don't sound like a closet drinker," Mel said as the cork popped easily.

"Not guilty, your honor. I go to sleep before I get drunk. I'm not much of a life of the party, I'm afraid."

"Me too. Terry used to get disgusted with me. Said it was a waste of money plying me with drink." Mel stopped, and her smile faltered a little. It seemed as though she hadn't thought about Terry since she arrived here. And yet, for the past six months she'd thought about nothing and no one else her entire waking day. Maybe getting away to Crys's farm *was* just what she needed to resolve her Terry issues and close that particular episode in her life.

Mel realized an uneasy silence had fallen between them, and she gathered her wayward thoughts. "But anyway, one or two glasses with dinner I can handle," she made herself add as lightly as she could.

"That's when I enjoy it, too," Crys said from across the breakfast bar.

Mel glanced at the label on the bottle. "Stanthorpe? I haven't tried anything from Queensland's Granite Belt, but I've heard Stanthorpe wines aren't bad."

"They're certainly getting more popular," Crys said. "I like some of them and, actually, that's my favorite," she added. "I went up to Stanthorpe and Girraween National Park a few weeks ago with some friends. We made a weekend of it, and even though it's getting pretty cold out there this time of year we had a great afternoon trekking around the wineries doing some serious tasting. Soon warmed us up."

She walked out of the kitchen and set their meal on the table as Mel poured the wine.

They sat down, and Mel exclaimed in delight. "Isn't this your famous apricot chicken?"

"Don't know about famous, but yes, it is apricot chicken. I still make it every so often."

"And I still love it. But nobody makes it quite as well as you do." Mel took a taste and sighed. "Mmm. That takes me back."

"I, well, I remembered you used to like it," Crys said, and their eyes met for long moments before Crys glanced back at her plate.

"This is really nice of you," Mel said sincerely.

Crys flushed a little. "Try the wine and see what you think."

Mel made an exaggerated show of holding her wineglass up to the light and then waving the glass under her nose before taking a sip. "Yes, a light fragrant bouquet," she said solemnly and grinned. "I don't know a lot about wines, but this tastes wonderful. Very more-ish."

"Well, drink up, eat, and be merry." Crys clinked her glass against Mel's. "And here's to an enjoyable stay."

"To an enjoyable stay," Mel repeated, and her eyes watched Crys over the rim of her glass.

Crys was the first to look away.

They ate in silence for a few minutes, and then Mel began to ask Crys about the farm. By the time they'd finished the main course and dessert of fresh fruit salad, Mel knew that although Crys grew and propagated lemon myrtle trees to harvest their essential oil, she was also experimenting with seedless

Davidson plums and that once a year she harvested broadleaf paspalum grass for its seeds.

However, the lemon myrtle was her main source of income. She also sold the leaves, which were dried and then steam-distilled for their oil.

"And there's a ready market for your produce overseas?" Mel asked as she helped Crys clear away the remnants of their meal.

"A very good market. Our Australian products are recognized for their pure quality. In fact, that's what keeps me going financially. The grass seed and the jams and jellies I make for the markets are just supplementary."

"How often do you go to market?" Mel asked, and Crys smiled.

"Usually twice a month. I could go every weekend if I had the energy. They rotate from place to place. I just do the two closest."

"And do you dress like a hippie and tell people's fortunes?" Mel teased.

"That's a preconceived idea if ever I heard one. You'll have to come along with me and broaden your horizons. Feel like some coffee?"

"Love some." Mel followed Crys back into the kitchen. "I'll wash the dishes while you get the coffee."

"You don't have to do that," Crys protested.

"Only fair. You cooked. I'll clear up. And there really aren't that many dishes," Mel added as she sought and found the dishwashing liquid. "You're a very tidy cook. I tend to use every bowl and piece of cutlery in the house."

"I'll remember that."

Soon they had retired to the living room with their mugs of coffee.

"Are you warm enough, or shall I light the fire?" Crys asked before she sat down.

"I'm okay." Mel chose the comfortable couch, arranging a couple of pillows at her back. "But the fire must be wonderful on a winter's evening."

"Wonderful and necessary." Crys relaxed into the matching chair opposite Mel. "It gets pretty cold here as the year wears on."

"I used to love the fireplace you had in the cottage in Brisbane, too," Mel said as she sipped her coffee. "Remember? We used to toast marshmallows."

"Singe them, you mean." Crys laughed. "I love an open fire. Although Paul used to say it was ridiculous having it when you only used it for a few months of the year. Paul was definitely not a romantic."

"I could never understand why you married him." Mel said the words before she thought about them, and she glanced at Crys, wondering if she'd offended her. "He was nice looking though," she added quickly.

"There're many of us taken in by a pretty face," Crys said lightly enough, but for a moment her comment hung between them, causing them both to pause. "But enough of that." Crys broke the uneasy silence. "Tell me about you, Mel. Are you and Marie-Therese working on a new book?"

Mel spluttered, and Crys leaned over, quickly taking her coffee mug from her until Mel had caught her breath.

"Okay?" Crys asked as she handed Mel back her coffee.

"Sorry. Must have gone down the wrong way," Mel

said, taking a cautious sip, knowing she was playing for time.

How was she going to answer Crys's casual question? Because she didn't really know if they *were* still a working partnership. When Terry had explained that she didn't want to be with Mel any more, she'd also said there was no need for their personal life to come between them professionally. Mel had angrily exclaimed her disbelief. And they hadn't spoken of a new book since then.

If Terry was the professional she professed to be, then surely she would have contacted Mel. But she hadn't. Unless Terry was waiting for Mel to contact her. Anyway, Mel was unsure how she felt about the situation. Could she still work with Terry? Or perhaps Terry had decided it was easier to find another artist to illustrate her books?

"Well, we haven't exactly started another book yet," she said vaguely. "At least, Marie-Therese hasn't given me a new story line. I guess I'll have to ring her soon and see how she's going. But I did a couple of freelance jobs before I left Melbourne."

"I loved the animal characters you did in the last one," Crys told her. "They're so lively and colorful. No wonder they're so popular."

"Thanks." Mel managed a smile. "I really enjoyed doing them."

"I saw you and Marie-Therese on the *Midday Show* last year. I don't see much daytime telly, but your mother rang me to tell me you were going to be on it." Crys's dark eyes scanned Mel's face. "You looked very striking on TV."

Mel flushed. "Who says the camera doesn't lie? I

had so much makeup on I thought my face would crack if I opened my mouth." Mel scratched her face in memory. "Made me so itchy I could barely put two thoughts together."

Crys laughed. "Rubbish! You came over very well. Very self-assured and professional."

"It was all an act." Mel grinned. "I was a quivering mass inside, believe me."

"And Marie-Therese seemed very nice, too. I could tell from the interview you had a good rapport with each other."

"We used to enjoy working together." Mel caught her breath when she realized she'd used the past tense, but Crys didn't seem to have picked up on it.

"I believe you met Marie-Therese at a party?"

"Yes. Years ago. We both moved in the art school crowd. It was a lucky meeting for both of us." Mel stifled a yawn, and Crys grimaced.

"Here I am talking your head off and you're exhausted. I'm sorry, Mel. Put it down to my rarely having a captive audience."

Mel laughed. "I'm all right. Really. It's just the pure country air. It was rainy and gray in Melbourne when I left, so all the sunshine since I came home has been fantastic."

They discussed the weather for a while, and Mel was amazed at how relaxed she was now becoming in Crys's company. But then, in the early days, she always had been. It was only after that stolen kiss that things had grown tense between them. If Mel could only put the memory of that out of her mind.

At that moment a loud mewing came from behind

the French doors. Crys stood up and crossed to open the door and in bounded two sleek cats. They stopped and eyed Mel with studied indifference.

"The black-and-white one is Paddy," Crys introduced. "And the larger tabby is Misty. You could say they run this place."

Mel made cooing noises, and the two cats merely strolled in the direction of their food bowls.

"They're just playing hard to get. In a day or so they'll be driving you mad. Every time you look like you're sitting down they'll be on your lap. Excuse me while I give them their dinner." Crys chided the cats good-naturedly and soon returned to sit down again.

"Did you catch up with your sister on your way through Brisbane?" she asked.

"No." Mel shook her head. "I haven't seen Amber and Adam since they came down to Melbourne last year."

And her sister and brother-in-law's visit had caused more than a little uneasiness between Mel and Terry. Terry had insisted on moving out to stay with friends, and Mel's so-called boyfriend, Terry, had supposedly gone home to Western Australia to see his parents.

Terry wouldn't even come along as Mel's writing partner to meet Amber and her family. The whole subterfuge had ruined Amber's visit for Mel. And later Mel had learned Terry had been with Maureen, the woman who became Terry's new lover.

"I was sorry I didn't make it to Amber's wedding," Crys was saying. "But Diane was too ill to travel. Was the wedding as amazing as your mother said it was?"

"And some." Mel rolled her eyes. "You missed the event of the century. Mum pulled out all stops for that wedding. I felt sorry for Amber. I can't believe she enjoyed it even if she said she did. I'd have eloped in the dead of night if I'd been her."

"And spoil all your mother's fun?" Crys laughed. "I can imagine how much Angela enjoyed playing mother of the bride."

"Oh, she had a ball. But I've told her there'll be no repeat performance with me, so she may as well get used to the idea."

Crys sobered. "I know you feel like that at the moment, Mel, but, well, that'll pass. Give it time."

"I guess so." And suddenly Mel found she wanted to confide in Crys, tell her everything. How betrayed she felt about Terry's perfidy. How much it hurt to know that someone she thought she knew wasn't that person. How much the pain lay heavily in her heart by the breaking of trust. But all that was treading on such dangerous ground.

Mel feigned a yawn. "You know, I do think I should call it a day," she said as evenly as she could. "What time do you usually get up?"

"Oh, I get up early, but you can sleep in as long as you like," Crys said as they walked down the hallway. "If I'm out in the shed when you wake up, just raid the fridge for breakfast. Oh, and close your bedroom door in case Paddy and Misty go in to try to con you into giving them a midnight snack."

Mel grinned. "Okay. See you in the morning. And, Crys, thanks."

"My pleasure." Crys smiled back and disappeared into her room.

* * * * *

Crys entered the restaurant and smiled as she joined her friends. The six of them met each Tuesday evening for a meal and a chat, and Crys really looked forward to it. Apart from her twice-monthly visits to the Sunday markets, it was her only social outing. Two in the group were a couple, and the others were single like Crys.

"Ah, the wanderer returns," said Margie Donovan, patting the vacant seat beside her for Crys to sit down.

"What happened to you last week?" Loretta Jones asked. "Please tell us you had a hot date."

"My little romantic." Billy Macklin patted Loretta's knee under the table. "She hasn't changed in the thirty years we've been together."

Loretta smiled at Billy before turning back to Crys. "So was it a hot date? Margie told us all you'd said was that something had come up. No explanations."

"She doesn't have to tell us everything," put in red-haired Sue Stevenson, at forty the youngest of the group. "Crys may not want to tell us." Sue ran a hand nervously through her tight curls.

"Or she might want to tell us it's none of our business," added Josey Rudd.

Crys laughed. "It's no mystery. When I rang Margie I got her machine and I just hate talking to answering machines. They're so off-putting."

"I'm with you there," Billy agreed. "Bloody awful things. So impersonal, and you end up either tongue-tied or babbling."

"So. What happened last Tuesday night?" Margie persisted. "You met this tall, dark strange woman who swept you off your feet and you decided she was more interesting than this sorry lot."

"I wish," quipped Crys, feeling suddenly a little warm. She shifted in her seat. "Actually I had, and still have, a houseguest."

"You have?" Josey Rudd's plump face beamed. "Why didn't you bring her along?"

"Yes, we could use some fresh blood." Margie rubbed her hands together and they all laughed.

"Now what makes you think it's a female house-guest?" Crys teased and watched the various and varied expressions of shock and disbelief on her friends' faces.

"You have a man in your house?" Sue asked incredulously, her blue eyes wide with horrified surprise.

"Not thinking of changing lanes at this time of life, are you, love?" Loretta inquired with mock seriousness.

"Bit late for that," Crys replied dryly. "No, my houseguest is a young woman, the daughter of an old friend."

"So why didn't you bring her along?" Josey repeated. "We'd have behaved ourselves. Well, we'd have tried," she added at the exclamations of skepticism.

"As I said, she's the daughter of a friend, a young daughter."

"Gee! Not only fresh blood but fresh young blood." Margie made drooling noises, and Sue frowned at her.

"You sound like a vampire." She shivered. "All that stuff scares me to death."

"How young are we talking here?" Josey asked quickly, steering Sue away from one of her lengthy monologues on things that go bump in the night.

"She's twenty-eight," Crys replied.

"Twenty-eight. A mere babe in arms," Loretta retorted. "I haven't seen twenty-eight for over thirty years. All the same, love," Loretta continued, "you could have brought her along. We wouldn't have minded, would we?"

"Well, I did consider bringing her, but she's not . . ." Crys paused.

"She's not one of us," Loretta finished for her. "Pity. But you know we're not exclusive."

"No. And we wouldn't hold it against her," Billy said quite seriously.

"Or hold ourselves against her, as much as we may want to," Margie added, and they all laughed again.

"She's just broken up with her boyfriend," Crys told them. "So she's a little down at the moment."

"And ripe for consolation," quipped Loretta.

Sue looked shocked again. "You're awful, Loretta. Do you know that?"

"I sure do, honey. I wouldn't want it any other way." Loretta grinned. "So how long will you be holding this young woman's hand, Crys?"

"I'm not sure." Crys shrugged. "Mel hasn't said how long she wants to stay, but she's been a great help this week."

"Mel? That's her name?" Margie frowned at Crys. "Isn't that your friend Angela's daughter? The one who writes the kids' books?"

"Yes. She's Angela's daughter and she's an illustrator."

"Oh, yes. I remember." Billy nodded. "You've told us about her before."

"Bring her along next week," Loretta directed lightly. "We had Josey's semi-straight friend last week."

"Loretta!" Josey admonished. "Ingrid's not semi-straight. She's just coming out. You know that's a difficult time."

"Loretta's problem is she popped out of her mother's womb clutching a rainbow flag," Margie said lightly. "And we all thought your Ingrid was very nice, Josey. It was a shame you didn't get to meet her, Crys."

"But she'll be here next week," Josey told them eagerly. "As you know we met at the hospital. We're on different wards and don't have our shifts in sync yet, so she can only get here every second week. But she enjoyed meeting you all, too."

"And have you two lovebirds done the dirty deed yet?" Loretta asked.

Billy groaned. "That's about as subtle as a hit over the head with a dead fish, Loretta." Billy retorted. "Give the girl a break. You've got her blushing."

Josey laughed good-naturedly. "For your information, Loretta, and not that I'm a kiss-and-tell, mind, but Ingrid and I went away for a couple of days at the end of last week. And that's all I'm saying."

At that moment the waitress came to take their orders, and there was a scrambling for menus.

* * * * *

Mel had a quick shower and pulled on a comfortable pair of track pants and a loose warm top. She curled up on the sofa and picked up the mystery novel she'd just started reading. The two cats immediately draped themselves all over her and juggled for position until the three of them were comfortable.

Absently Mel stroked the cats' warm fur. She felt as though she'd been here with Crys for months rather than a little more than a week. It all seemed so right somehow.

She was even helping Crys with the seedlings now, and today Crys had taught her how to drive the cantankerous old tractor, which caused them both a good deal of merriment. And next week they were going to harvest the paspalum seed in Crys's lower paddock. Crys said she usually made a day of it and took a picnic lunch to have by the river. Mel was really looking forward to it.

She yawned, feeling a pleasant tiredness in her muscles. The physical work she'd been doing made her feel far more alive than she'd felt in ages.

Each evening she and Crys took turns cooking dinner, and Mel knew she was eating far more sensibly and regularly than she had been. Since arriving at the farm she'd lost that pinched look, and she felt she was looking more like her old self.

And she was sleeping wonderfully well — apart from the occasional wakeful moments when she imagined that she was not alone in the comfortable double bed and that Crys had slipped quietly between the sheets, her warm naked body pressed close to Mel's.

Mel groaned, and Misty raised her head and looked expectantly up at her.

"It's okay, Puss," she said softly. "I'm just thinking about taking liberties with your owner. Well, actually, I was imagining her taking liberties with me. Either way, I wouldn't say no." Mel sighed. "Ungrateful wretch, aren't I? Taking her hospitality and repaying it by lusting after her incredibly sexy body."

Mel paused and grimaced. Sitting here on her own thinking licentious thoughts obviously wasn't helping, let alone the fact that she was talking to the cat. What did she expect? That the cat might all of a sudden tell her to throw discretion to the wind and jump Crys's bones?

"And what do you think your mistress would think about that, Puss? If I jumped her gorgeous bones?"

The cat blinked appraisingly, and Mel sighed loudly.

"So here I am lusting after my mother's best friend and discussing the merits of it with a cat. I'm slipping from the sublime to the ridiculous."

So much for sitting here on her own. Maybe she should have gone out to dinner with Crys, met her friends. But that could have been complicated, too.

Although Crys hadn't said so, Mel surmised her friends were lesbians, and if they'd asked questions Mel would have to have been on her guard. And good friends, friends Crys had told Mel she'd known for years, would be the first to notice that Mel was feeling more than a casual friendship for Crys. Yes, it was all too complicated. Far better to have stayed home.

Paddy got up and went to check his food bowl, and Mel stretched out more comfortably on the couch. Misty took advantage of the situation and settled across Mel's thighs. Determinedly, Mel opened her book and tried to pick up the threads of her story.

An hour later the book had slipped to the floor and Mel was in that transitory state between being awake and asleep.

She was walking along the river with Terry. They stopped, sat side by side on a bench, huddling as close together as they dared. Terry had brought along some bread and they fed the ducks, talked, and laughed. Then they moved on until they found a tree with overhanging branches and they slipped beneath them, strained against each other, exhilarated and frustrated by their lack of privacy. Until Terry took Mel's arm and hurried her back to their small flat and the wonderful seclusion of it.

Almost before the door was closed, Terry had pulled off Mel's coat and slid her hands beneath Mel's sweater, her cold fingers making Mel squeal and try to escape. And then they were on the narrow bed and Terry was slowly driving her mad with her fingers and tongue, teasing Mel until she begged for release.

Mel stirred, suddenly perturbed, disquiet clutching at her. She frowned. She wanted Terry to hold her close, stroke her hair, talk to her, but Terry was moving away as she usually did.

Mel murmured softly. She'd often felt this slight sense of loss, of unfulfillment somehow, after they'd made love.

No. She moved and the cat protested. No, she was being absurd. She was only dreaming. They had had a fantastic love life. Exciting. Exhilarating. And all orchestrated by Terry.

Mel frowned again. She didn't want to think about all this. It was old news. She wanted to wake up, get herself out of this disturbing dream, but it held her captive, and she was too drowsy to pull herself awake.

She would have liked to drift off to a place where she was with Crys, where Crys was reaching out, where she felt the softness of Crys's skin, her warmth.

And then she felt the light touch of a hand on her head, brushing over her hair so gently she wondered if she was imagining it. The hand moved and cool skin feathered her cheek, lightly tracing the line of her jaw.

CHAPTER FIVE

Mel's taut muscles, muscles she hadn't realized were so tense, slowly relaxed, and she sighed.

"Mel." A low, liquid voice said her name, the sound of it reaching out, enveloping her, cocooning her in a delicious warmth.

"Mel." There it was again. So wonderfully soothing. So sensual.

Mel's lips twitched. She felt a small smile play around the corners of her mouth, and she murmured her pleasure. She could drift like this forever. But she wanted more, knew there was more. Her eyelids fluttered, revealed the back of a strong hand as those cool fingers continued to stroke her cheek.

And there was a dark head, the curve of a strong jaw, a small nose, the contours of a determined chin, and a soft, smiling, so inviting mouth.

Mel was almost overcome with the desire to touch those lips with her own. She stirred and began to raise herself, her fingers taking hold of that gentling hand, the pad of her thumb stroking the exposed palm.

"Crys?" she said sleepily, and felt her body arch toward the other woman. She wanted to pull Crys down on top of her, feel the soft, so feminine curves meld with her own.

"Mel? Wake up, love. You'd be more comfortable in bed," Crys's deep voice said above her.

Only if you're there, too. The words trembled on Mel's lips as she came fully awake, stopping herself just in time. What if she'd said those words? Had she actually voiced them? Her eyes opened wide and she studied Crys's face, but there was no horror, no indication that she had said anything untoward.

Mel reluctantly released Crys's hand and pushed herself into a sitting position. Misty protested with a loud and indignant mew.

Crys had straightened and moved a few feet away from the couch. "I see Misty has claimed squatter's rights," she said lightly as Mel swung her feet to the floor.

"She, um, she does a pretty good job as a hot water bottle."

Crys laughed. "That she does."

"Did you have a good evening?" Mel asked,

ostensibly rubbing her eyes with her hand, hoping Crys wouldn't notice the warmth she knew had colored her face.

"Wonderful. The meal was delicious. However —" Crys made a face — "I was soundly chastised for not bringing you along with me. They're a really nice group of women."

"Are they lesbians?" Mel heard herself ask.

Crys paused slightly before she replied. "Yes. Yes, they are. But we don't —"

"I know." Mel stood up. "It doesn't matter. I was just, well, just curious, that's all." She shrugged. "I'm sure I'd like them if you do. Maybe I could go with you next week. That is, if you go."

Crys smiled vaguely. "That would be fine. They'd all enjoy meeting you."

"Mmm," Mel murmured noncommittally.

"Well, I guess we should turn in." It was Crys's turn to stifle a yawn.

"Do you want some coffee?" Mel was suddenly loath for them to be separated, especially by the wall between their bedrooms.

"No, thanks." Crys shook her head. "I had some coffee after dinner. Any more and I won't be able to sleep. How about you?"

"Oh, no. I'm fine." Mel glanced at her watch. "Coffee this late would keep me up, too."

They walked toward their rooms.

Perhaps they should both have coffee, Mel contemplated hysterically, and stay awake and make love till dawn. Mel's body heat increased rapidly at the recalcitrant thought.

"Maybe you'll be able to return to your dream,"

Crys said lightly. "I was disinclined to wake you, you looked so peaceful. Do you remember what you were dreaming about?"

"Oh. No. Not really." Mel guiltily stretched the truth. "So it can't have been that good."

Crys laughed softly. "Seems not. See you in the morning."

Mel nodded and went into her room.

Did she remember what she'd been dreaming about? Oh, yes. She remembered all right. What an understatement! she derided herself as she sank onto the side of the bed. If only she could pick up the dream from when Crys's hands touched her face and then have the dream continue on from there. Or better still, Mel reflected recklessly, make the dream an erotic reality.

She swallowed. That wouldn't be sensible, she told herself. All this fantasizing was only making her awareness of the other woman more intense by the minute. And it was already becoming harder for Mel to keep some distance between them.

Crys took a quick shower, donned the long-sleeved T-shirt she wore to bed, brushed her teeth, and ran a comb through her hair. Then she stretched out beneath the doona, the thick eiderdown comforter.

She felt decidedly unsettled. And whose fault was that? she asked herself irritatedly. She'd brought it all on herself. She'd only meant to lightly touch Mel so she'd wake up without getting a fright.

Bad move, Crys, she admonished herself. What had possessed her to touch Mel the way she had? Instead of gently patting her awake, she'd allowed that fleeting touch to linger for far too long. Mel could so easily have misconstrued.

Crys laughed softly in self-derision. If she was totally honest with herself she'd have welcomed any misconstruction on Mel's part. Anything to hold Mel's beautiful body in her arms. Crys moaned softly, calling herself all kinds of a fool.

When she'd walked into the house and found Mel asleep on the couch, she'd stood quietly and watched her, allowed herself the luxury of letting her gaze linger on the young woman.

Her beautiful face, softened so delightfully in sleep. Her firm breasts, flat stomach. The exciting spot where her long legs met . . . How she wished she could kneel down, bury her face in the softness, the heady feminine aroma of Mel's body.

Crys shifted agitatedly in her bed. For heaven's sake! She was allowing her errant thoughts to get way out of hand. And it had to stop. Yet how she wanted . . .

All right! Go ahead and face it, she reproached herself. What did she want? She wanted to hold Mel close, let her fingers and tongue explore her, make long, sweet love to her.

Crys's body responded to her libidinous musing. Her nipples prickled to attention, and an arrow of arousal centered between her legs. For the first time since she'd lost Diane, she actually felt a burning, inciting need to make love with another woman.

But why Mel Jamieson? she asked herself agitatedly. She'd come into contact with any number of women in the past five years. In an offhand way she'd noticed these women were intelligent and attractive, but none of them had stirred her senses the way Mel did.

Perhaps it was simply a normal part of her healing process after the loss of Diane, and Mel just happened to come along at the right time. Or maybe it was just her hormones beginning to play up. She was forty-two, she reminded herself. She could expect bodily changes as she entered menopause.

But all that aside, putting forward reasons why she might be attracted to Mel didn't exactly clarify or solve the problem. The bottom line was that she couldn't allow herself to act on her oh-so-incendiary impulses. It just wasn't possible.

But why wasn't it conceivable? a small yearning voice said from deep down inside her. She, Crys, was an adult, and so was Mel. They were both free to do as they pleased. But, of course, another small part of Crys that clutched at rationality thrust forward all the reasons why she couldn't permit herself to follow up on the dictates of her body.

She was fourteen years older than Mel, old enough to know better than to take advantage of someone so much younger than she was. Mel was her best friend's daughter. And she was straight. It was mega-foolish getting involved with a straight woman, Crys told herself forcefully. That was one of the rules of the sisterhood, if such rules actually existed. And if they didn't exist, Crys decided peevishly, then they should.

Of course, all this was pure fantasy, existing only in her apparently very vivid imagination. She knew if she let her guard down, allowed Mel to see just how attracted to the younger woman she was, then Mel was more than likely to run screaming. Even if Mel had been confused about her sexuality as a teenager, Mel had been living with a man for the past six years. Elementary, my dear Watson, Crys told herself scornfully.

But what if Mel was still interested in . . . ? Crys sought the words she hardly dared even think. What if Mel wanted to explore her sexuality? Crys cringed at her trite turn of phrase and shifted exasperatedly in her bed. She was beginning to sound like some sort of pseudopsychoanalyst.

Yet deep down a small part of her clung to the concept. It was a possibility, wasn't it? If Mel . . .

Crys angrily turned over, plumping her pillow with more than necessary vigor.

And wouldn't that be worse? she asked herself brutally. If she, Crys, was just an experiment to Mel, one she wanted to pick up where she'd left off all those years ago . . . Crys sank back into her bed. Somehow that thought was completely and utterly devastating, and she couldn't or wouldn't admit to herself just why this was so.

They headed off to the lower paddock. Crys was driving the tractor with the seed-harvesting implement attached and Mel carefully followed her in the truck. The old tractor spluttered and coughed, and Mel was amazed it actually kept going.

Surely Crys would have to consider getting a new one soon. Mel had no idea how much such a piece of machinery cost to buy, but she suspected they weren't cheap. Maybe Crys couldn't afford it. Mel's mother had said Crys was hardly well off.

Mel sighed as she glimpsed the valley through the trees. A light mist was gradually dissipating as the sun rose. It seemed everyone's life was fraught in some way.

They turned left and followed the bitumen road for a short distance before taking what was little more than a rough track through high grasses down to the right. The track branched, and Crys took the right fork, heading back toward a sagging iron gate in a barbed wire fence that was barely visible in the undergrowth.

Crys climbed down from the tractor and opened the gate, then she drove the tractor far enough through to allow the truck to follow. Crys walked up to join Mel, raising her voice above the irregular chugging of the idling tractor.

"I'll close the gate and then we'll park the truck over under the trees. It'll be cooler for you to sit there than out here in the full sun."

Mel nodded, and Crys swung the gate closed behind the truck. As Crys passed her Mel called out, "And I'll close the gate next time to save you getting down off the tractor."

Crys smiled and waved, and they continued along the fence line toward the trees that followed the creek Mel had seen from Crys's veranda.

They started when Crys decided the dew was gone from the grass and, although Crys protested, Mel took her turn on the noisy machine as it whipped the seed into the box. When she rested, Mel took out the sketchbook she'd brought with her and tried to capture the lines and angles of Crys at work, patiently following the row cut back and forward along the length of the paddock.

Taking the last turn on the tractor before lunchtime, Mel was more than ready for a break so she could sit down on something that didn't shake every inch of her.

"I feel like I'm still moving standing still," she said to Crys.

"Well, I did warn you." Crys frowned. "You don't have to do this, Mel. I'm used to it, and I know how tiring it is. Not that I don't appreciate your help. I really do. I'm way ahead of schedule, and I'll be finished long before I normally am when I do it all myself. You can still go home and relax for the afternoon and I'll finish up."

Mel grinned. "What, and miss the fabulous picnic lunch we packed?"

"I meant after lunch," Crys explained, and Mel shook her head.

"I'm fine, Crys. I promise I'll tell you if it all gets too much for me. Okay?"

"All right." Crys agreed reluctantly.

"So, where shall we have our lunch? And can it be preferably somewhere that doesn't move?"

"If you don't mind a short walk, we could go down by the river." Crys grinned. "Unless running water constitutes moving."

"That I can live with."

"Okay. Let's go. Just watch your step down this bank." Crys led the way, and Mel followed her down a rough, irregular track.

They picked their way through a group of straggly trees, and Mel could hear the sound of cascading water. She exclaimed in surprise when they came out into the sunshine again and found they were on a small grassy bank overlooking a crystal-clear stream tumbling over smooth, round rocks.

"This is the creek I can see from your place, isn't it?" she asked, and Crys laughed softly.

"This creek is the beginning of the mighty Tweed River."

Mel paused in the act of setting down the small cooler of food she'd been carrying. "You mean the Tweed River I crossed over on my way down? This is it?"

"Sure is. Actually this is the South Arm. It rises in the Tweed Range southwest of Mount Warning. The other two tributaries that join with this one and go on to form the Tweed River begin in the McPherson Ranges."

"Amazing." Mel looked at the water with new eyes. "I didn't realize. You'd hardly believe it when you see how wide it is closer to the coast."

"If it was summertime we could go a little farther along the creek and have a reviving swim. It's a bit wider and deeper there and makes a wonderful swimming hole."

"We can't today?" Mel looked at the cool water. "I'm warm enough after all that work to take a refreshing dip."

Crys shivered. "You might think so but, believe me, the water's freezing."

Mel shrugged. "Oh, well. Pity. I didn't bring my swimsuit anyway."

"If you want to swim you don't have to stand on ceremony with me." Crys was spreading out the old blanket she carried. "This is pretty private and no one ever comes down this far, so feel free to skinny-dip if you want to."

Mel sent her a quick look and her body tensed, her nerve endings tingling. She had a vivid picture of herself and Crys, naked, splashing in the cool water. She swallowed as her heart rate increased threefold.

"But I think you should give it the toe or finger test before you decide," Crys was adding. "As I said, it's pretty cold this time of year."

Mel stepped closer to the water and pretended to regard the babbling stream. In truth she was waiting for her excited flush to subside before she rejoined the other woman.

"It does look cold," she said as evenly as she could.

"Chicken." Crys chuckled softly. "I guess we'll have to wait till the weather warms up before we consider any swimming, clothed or not. In summer it's magic. Well, how about some lunch?"

Mel murmured noncommittally, not meeting Crys's gaze as she busied herself unclipping the lid of the cooler. If she didn't banish from her mind all these graphic thoughts of Crys's naked body, she'd be incapable of speaking coherently, let alone trying to eat her lunch. Resolutely Mel lifted the top of the cooler. There, nestled on their picnic lunch, was a small bottle of wine. She lifted it out in surprise.

"I didn't see you put this in."

Crys smiled. "I thought some wine would be nice. I'm limiting myself to one glass, though. Any more and I'll probably go to sleep."

"Great." Mel handed Crys the wine and two plastic wineglasses and continued unpacking their picnic.

They had a crisp tossed salad with a tangy dressing, corn, chicken, and crusty bread. And there was fresh fruit for afterward.

Mel set out the two plates. "Shall I dish up?" she asked. Crys nodded as she uncorked the wine bottle and poured out two glasses.

Soon they were eating enthusiastically, and Mel murmured appreciatively as she took a sip of wine.

"This is delicious. I didn't realize I was so hungry," she said. "Apart from that, I love picnics."

"You always did," Crys said lightly.

"Remember we always went to Colleges Crossing?" Mel said as old memories rose.

Crys nodded. "I have a photograph of us all taken on one of our many jaunts up there."

"You do? You'll have to show me one day." Mel laughed. "We had great fun."

Crys grimaced. "Most of the time."

Mel's smile faltered. "You mean it was fun when Paul didn't come with us. I remember that too."

"I shouldn't have —" Crys sighed and nodded. "You were just a child. I didn't know if you would have noticed Paul's moodiness. He could be a real wet blanket when he tried."

"Well, I do remember it was better when he didn't come with us. That's awful, isn't it?"

"But true," Crys agreed. "Paul was a very unhappy person. I didn't realize when I met him how moody and self-focused he really was. Of course, I wasn't the woman he thought he was getting either, so that didn't help."

"Mum was the only one who could coax him out of a bad mood."

"Yes." Crys shook her head sadly. "I guess Paul should have married someone like Angela. I'm afraid I let him down badly."

"From what I remember he didn't do much to help himself," Mel defended Crys.

"Maybe not." Crys shrugged. "Well, anyway, that's all water under the bridge, as they say. But those picnics at Colleges Crossing with you all were pretty great, weren't they?"

Mel grinned. "They sure were."

"You were a frightful tease back then," Crys continued. "Remember the day you tipped me off the inner tube and the strap on my swimsuit broke?" Crys chuckled. "God, I was mortified. Squatting beneath the water with one boob floating free. Squatting beneath the very clear, almost transparent water, I might add," she said with feeling, and Mel actually flushed at the memory.

Especially after she'd been imagining Crys naked in this creek only a short time ago. And Mel knew she remembered that particular afternoon very well. She'd been absolutely awed that day staring at the perfect, full shape of Crys's breast. She must have been about twelve or thirteen at the time, and she was still as flat chested herself as she'd always been.

As she'd stood in the water near Crys, Mel had had to fight the urge to reach out, touch Crys's body, and bury her face in the damp softness of it. And she could feel again the confusing emotions — the mixture of excitement and shame — that moment had aroused within her.

Crys had looked so very beautiful. Just recalling it now caused a tightening between Mel's legs. She

79

looked up at Crys again, and the other woman was still smiling, apparently oblivious of Mel's licentious thoughts.

"I had the darnedest trouble trying to cover my modesty until your mother took pity on me and saved the day with a large, enveloping towel."

Mel made herself laugh lightly. "Mum to the rescue again."

"Exactly," said Crys with feeling. "Paul was livid with me and later he gave me a long-winded lecture about being a lady and behaving in a seemly manner befitting my position as his wife. We had a huge fight. But then again, fighting was all we seemed to do."

Mel sighed. "You know it was the same with Dad and Mum before they got a divorce," she said softly. "Not that Dad was as bad as Paul, but since Dad married Cindy he's been a different person. It's amazing how life changes your whole personality, isn't it?"

"It changes some people's personalities. It appears to depend on the person."

Mel gave that some thought and then nodded. "I guess you're right. Mum was unhappy with Dad, too, but it didn't make her moody and irritable with everyone else." Mel looked at Crys. "Or you. You were never like that either."

Crys gave a crooked smile. "Oh, I had my moments, as Paul would no doubt tell you."

"But you were always okay with us," Mel said.

Crys looked off into the distance. "Being with you, with Angela and you and Amber, was often my only salvation," she said softly. "You made life bearable for me."

"It was that bad?" Mel asked incredulously.

"Pretty much so. Paul was" — Crys grimaced — "manipulative, controlling, mentally abusive. And I gave him that power over me because, right or wrong, I always felt guilty for marrying him." She glanced back at Mel. "Your mother made me see what was happening, helped me get everything back into perspective. She's a good friend."

Mel nodded. "It must have been hard for you."

They were silent for long moments and then Crys shrugged again. "Well, that's in the past now, and we don't want to put a complete damper on the rest of the day. Let's have a change of subject." She dug into the cooler. "How about an apple?"

Mel took the fruit and absently polished the rosy skin on the leg of her jeans. "I know Mum's been great, but Mum and I . . ." She paused, seeking the right words. "We haven't always seen eye to eye."

Crys grinned. "That's an understatement." She sobered. "But your mother does love you, Mel."

"I know. I guess we're just different people. Maybe she should have had two daughters like Amber."

"Rubbish!" Crys exclaimed. "Your mother loves you as you are. Both of you."

And would she still love me if she knew I was a lesbian? Mel wanted to ask.

"It's difficult realizing your kids have grown up," Crys continued. "But she's very proud of you."

Mel nodded. "I know she is." And she did know that. "But she doesn't really know me," Mel said carefully. "I mean, I haven't lived at home for ten years or so. I sort of feel I've, well, grown away from her."

"Not really away from her. You've just grown up, and as you said, made your own life. But you're still basically you, Mel. That never changes." Crys leaned forward and gave Mel a slight shove. "Unless you've developed into a secret homicidal maniac or something," she added teasingly.

Mel laughed despite herself, her mood lightening. "No. I'll admit I felt like slipping over the edge a couple of times, but my innate goodness must have held me back. What do you think?"

"I think it must have." Crys lay back and tried to settle the cooler lid under her head as a pillow. "Mmm, don't you love the smell of freshly cut grass? And the food and the wine and the good company have made me sleepy." She moved the cooler lid and grimaced.

"That doesn't look very comfortable," Mel said.

Crys squirmed again. "It isn't but in lieu of a soft pillow . . ."

Before she thought about it, Mel pushed herself to her hands and knees and moved over behind Crys. She sat down and removed the cooler lid, sliding her long legs under Crys's head in place of the lid.

"There. That should be more comfortable." Mel looked down, her eyes met Crys's, and that same tingling of awareness sprang so easily to the surface again.

CHAPTER SIX

Mel and Crys arrived home from the lower paddock and took much-needed showers. Tomorrow they'd sift the seed to remove blades of grass and insects before spreading the seed out to dry. Now, after a light meal, they were sitting in the lounge.

Crys had picked up the newspaper and was reading the day's news, but Mel felt jumpy and disoriented. She had been since those few seconds when Crys's head had been resting in Mel's lap and Crys had looked up at her with those unfathomable dark eyes. It seemed to Mel that every minute nerve ending in her body had sprung into absolute alert mode. And stayed there.

Looking back, Mel couldn't have told how long they'd stared into each other's eyes, but just as Mel went to twine her fingers in Crys's thick, graying hair and lower her mouth to Crys's lips, Crys had broken that disturbing eye contact.

"Well, it is much more comfortable," she'd said easily. "But just tell me when I cut off your circulation and your leg goes to sleep." And then Crys had closed her eyes.

Mel's hand had fallen back onto the blanket, but her body had continued to clamor its charged arousal. Cut off her circulation? Mel could almost laugh at that. Her circulation had gone into overdrive, her blood rushing around her body in an unequivocal frenzy.

They'd stayed like that for what seemed to Mel like an eternity, Crys apparently relaxed and Mel growing more tense by the second. In the periphery of her senses Mel took in the surrounding sounds, the rush of water over rocks, the buzz of busy insects, the chattering of birds in the trees. She saw the clear blue sky, the variegated greens of the trees and undergrowth. And she felt the cool breeze on her heated skin.

Yet Mel's entire being was focused on Crys, on her nearness, on the weight of her head on Mel's thigh, the sight of strands of Crys's thick hair shifting in the wind. Mel's narrowed gaze took in the length of Crys's body stretched out on the blanket, her booted feet crossed at the ankles, her jeans-clad legs, rounded hips, and narrow waist, and the swell of her full breasts molded by her dark blue T-shirt.

Mel could even convince herself she could see the outline of Crys's nipples, and her fingers yearned to reach out, tease those dusky peaks into hard nubs. And Mel swallowed convulsively, her mouth dry.

With her entire body as taut as a guitar string, Mel decided she could bear it no longer. She thought she'd go mad if she didn't make some move. Take Crys in her arms. Get up and walk away. Anything.

And just then Crys stretched, pushed herself into a sitting position, and broke that so emotive contact.

"I guess this isn't getting the paddock finished," she said ruefully.

Mel pulled her legs up close to her body, clasped her arms around her knees. "It's so peaceful here, isn't it?" she said lamely, still so very aware of the heated imprint of Crys's head lingering on her thigh. "But I suppose you're right. We should get back to work."

"It's my turn on the tractor anyway." Crys stood up and arched her back, causing her breasts to thrust out against her T-shirt.

Mel couldn't help but stare at the line of Crys's body, and she grew hot again.

"You might as well relax for a while longer," Crys was continuing, unaware of Mel's covert regard. "I'll get back to it." Then she was walking away, climbing up on the tractor, and disappearing from sight. As the tractor engine spluttered to life, Mel slowly released the breath she was holding.

Now, after sitting in the living room across from Crys, trying to find some interest in a farming magazine rather than Crys's body, Mel decided she had to distract herself. She'd write a couple of postcards to her young nephew and niece. She'd bought the cards at Burleigh Heads and Aaron enjoyed such things to take to preschool for show-and-tell. Two-year-old Amanda liked anything her big brother liked.

"Damn. My pen's just run out." Mel glared at the offending ballpoint.

"There's a box of them in the drawer over there." Crys turned the page of the newspaper, and Mel got up and walked over to the sideboard.

"In this drawer here?"

"Mmm. Top one."

Mel opened the drawer and shifted some papers. There was the box of pens resting on top of a photograph in a gold frame. Before she'd considered it might be intruding on Crys's privacy, Mel pulled the photograph out and stared down at the youthful face smiling up at her. The scrawled message and signature were plainly legible.

All my love, Diane.

So this was Diane King. Although Mel had known of Diane's existence in Crys's life, she had never met Crys's partner. Crys had introduced Diane to Mel's mother, but all Angela had said was that Diane seemed a nice person. And later, when Mel had developed her crush on Crys, she'd felt a burning jealousy of the other woman who was only a name associated with the scandal that had surrounded Crys.

Mel gazed curiously at the photo. Diane's was a conventionally pretty face, gamine, Mel guessed you'd call it, and her fairish hair was cut short, feathering her brow and cheeks.

"Where did you meet her?" Mel didn't realize she'd actually spoken the words until she heard her own voice. She cringed, not believing she could be so insensitive.

She didn't know if Crys still found it painful to talk about Diane. She certainly didn't mention her very often.

The paper rustled, and Mel turned to face Crys, the photograph still in her hands. She shot a quick glance at the other woman.

Crys met her gaze for long moments, and then she looked casually back at the newspaper.

"Diane and I met at school," she said evenly.

"At Somerville House?" Mel said softly. Crys nodded. "That's where you first met Mum, too, wasn't it? Did she know Diane as well back then?"

Crys shook her head. "No. Your mother had left school before Diane transferred there. Your mother was a senior when I started at Somerville, and Diane was nearly a year younger than I was."

"Oh. She's" — Mel swallowed — "she was very attractive."

"Yes. She was." Crys sighed softly. "That photo was taken after we left school. She must have been about eighteen."

"You . . . were you . . . ?" Mel flushed, her throat closing, and Crys folded her newspaper and set it aside.

"Were Diane and I lovers back then?" Crys finished for her. Mel nodded.

For some reason Mel could hear her heartbeats thumping in her chest.

"Yes, we were," Crys continued. "We had been for a couple of years, while we were still at school, and afterward we shared a flat. I worked and Diane went to teachers' training college."

"But you, well, got married." Mel voiced something that had bothered her for years.

"A lot of people, both men and women, get married when they shouldn't, Mel," Crys said dryly and shrugged. "Yes, I married Paul."

Mel watched Crys's fingers worry at the seam in her jeans. Then she sighed and looked across at Mel.

"I was nineteen, nearly twenty, when I got married. That was three months after Diane was posted to teach at a school in the country and decided it would be a good time for us to go our separate ways." Crys gave a soft humorless laugh. "Well, eventually it was a mutual decision.

"We both felt the need to conform. And maybe we got tired of making excuses, fabricating absent boyfriends. I don't know. I guess I made a lot of mistakes when I was younger."

Mel tried for a light note. "Don't we all?"

Their eyes met, and Mel blushed hotly. Was Crys remembering Mel's youthful indiscretion?

"So you must have been married for some time before you moved in next door to us?" she continued quickly. Crys nodded.

"About five years or so. And things weren't too great between Paul and me even then. On top of everything we'd both wanted to start a family and hadn't had any success with that, so I guess we were both a bit stressed. What with one thing and another it put quite a strain on our already shaky marriage. We'd also separated twice during that time."

Crys looked away again. "And the year before Paul and I came to live near you, Diane had called me. She'd been transferred back to the city and wanted us to get back together."

Mel's eyebrows rose in surprise. "Had Diane married or anything?"

"No. She'd been engaged but was sensible enough to see what a mistake she'd be making if she went ahead with it. Unlike I did. She'd had a couple of relationships with women, but she told me none of them meant as much to her as I did.

"I knew I was still in love with her, so I decided to be honest and told Paul I wanted a divorce and why. I thought he'd be angry, but he wasn't. Well, I thought he wasn't." She shook her head. "I must have been living with my head in the clouds. Now I look back I can see he was absolutely livid with me, with both of us. But he hid that so well. He pretended he was all wounded but understanding, and he said he wanted us to stay friends.

"I ended up feeling guiltier by the minute. Then one night Paul called at Diane's flat. I'd left Paul and had moved in with her by then. Well, Paul wanted to see me about something, I can't remember what. One thing led to another, and Diane and I argued and, well, to cut a long story short, Diane accused me of caring more for him than I did for her, and we had the most devastating row in front of Paul.

"Diane left and Paul consoled me." She gave another short laugh. "With hindsight I can see he was a master manipulator. He somehow talked me into coming back to him, giving our marriage another try. I told him I'd think about it."

Crys shook her head. "I was pulled in two directions. When I tried to discuss it with Diane, she called me all kinds of a fool for even considering going back to Paul. In the end things were unbearable between Diane and me, and Paul, well, he was waiting patiently in the wings."

Crys grimaced and looked at Mel. "I know all this

makes me sound very weak and indecisive, but I was young, and times were a little different then. I'm not proud of my decision to go back to Paul, Mel. I'm afraid I did him a great disservice by doing so." She sighed. "At the time I was so confused. But I really did want to make a fresh start, and I wanted a family."

"So you bought the cottage next door to ours?" Mel said, and Crys nodded.

"My aunt had just died and left me some money, so Paul and I bought the house. I hadn't seen your mother since she'd left Somerville, and then it turned out she was living next door. It was an amazing coincidence, wasn't it?"

Mel smiled. "Mum once said she couldn't believe it when she realized you'd gone to the same school and that you remembered each other. She said you hadn't seen each other for about thirteen years."

"At least that long." Crys smiled at the memory. "We became good friends. As I said, your mother saved my sanity on countless occasions. I don't know what I'd have done without her to talk to."

"Did my mother know?" Mel asked softly. "I mean, when you moved in, did she know about you and Diane?"

"Not about Diane and me exactly." Crys made a face. "But she knew about a certain incident at school. Another girl and I were caught kissing in the sports room. It was a huge scandal at the time. We nearly got expelled. When I turned up next door, safely married, your mother thought I'd grown out of it." Crys laughed softly. "And talking about the incident at school, I once accused Diane of only seeking me out because she'd heard the rumor and been warned about my, shall we say, tendencies. She said she didn't."

"So you were notorious," Mel said lightly. Crys laughed again.

"You could say that. At any rate, when your mother and I met up again all those years later it wasn't exactly a terrible surprise to Angela when I eventually confessed about Diane." Crys shrugged. "Maybe your mother expected as much. Scandal did seem to follow me."

"What? Kissing a girl when you were a kid? That was hardly a scandal," Mel reassured her. "You wouldn't have been the only one."

"I was the only one caught. I guess I must have been about twelve or thirteen. And in those days it was a scandal, believe me." Crys looked down at her hands. "And I suppose you remember my very public divorce."

Mel nodded. "Yes." She frowned slightly. "But I thought you and Diane broke up before you came to live near us."

"We did. But Diane phoned me when David was going on two years old. I was really surprised to hear from her, and I agreed to meet her for lunch. It was good to see her again." Crys absently rubbed her forehead. "We fell into the habit of having lunch together every week. I'd take David with me and we'd talk. That's all it was." Crys shrugged.

"Funny, isn't it? It was all so innocent then. And it was David who guilelessly cooked our goose. He was just starting to string words together. Paul and I were having dinner one night and David said, as clear as a bell, that Auntie Di liked chocolate cake."

Crys made a negating movement with her hands. "Paul went ballistic. He accused me of having an affair with Diane and swore he'd take David away from me. He was as good as his word. And the rest, as they say, is history."

"Do you ever see David?" Mel asked hesitantly.

Crys shook her head sadly. "No. In the beginning I used to. The court's ruling was that I would have visitation in a public place, with Paul in attendance. It was harrowing. And it upset David far too much. It was tearing him in two. I knew Paul would never relent, so I caved in to him again. He took David to Sydney to live near his grandmother, and he graciously let me keep the house."

Crys paused. "David would be sixteen now. I live in hope that one day he might want to see me again. I've written him letters I'll give him if, when he does."

"I'm sorry." Mel wondered how Crys had coped with it all.

"Yes. So am I. Maybe I'd have handled it differently now. I don't know. But we can't turn back the clock."

"No, I guess we can't." Mel agreed. She put the photograph back in the drawer. "You stayed on in the house on your own. I mean, why didn't you and Diane, after the divorce, why didn't you get together?"

"Paul saw to it that that was one of the stipulations of the visitation rights. I couldn't bring David into a situation that might morally corrupt him. I had to be so careful."

"Could they specify that?" Mel asked incredulously.

Crys grimaced. "Oh, yes. A court that decides a manipulative, alcoholic father is a better role model for a child than a lesbian mother can do anything," Crys said with what was obviously deep-seated bitterness.

"It's unbelievable." Mel sat down in the chair opposite Crys.

"That it was. But after Paul took David down south, what was the point? Diane had lost her job teaching because of the court case. Of course that wasn't the reason given to her for her contract not being renewed but . . . Anyway, that's when we decided to get back together, buy the farm, and make a new start. I sold the cottage and we moved down here."

Crys stood up and walked across to the darkened window, staring out into the night. "We were just starting to make a go of the place when Diane got sick."

"It doesn't seem fair." Mel stood up too, wanting to cross to Crys, put her arms around her, offer comfort. But unsure of Crys's reaction, she stayed where she was. "I mean, after all you'd been through to be together."

Crys was silent, and Mel took a couple of steps toward her, stopping when the other woman sighed.

"No. It certainly wasn't fair," Crys agreed flatly. "It's such a cruel disease. It seemed that one day Diane was a fit, vital, healthy person, full of life. And the next day she was —" Crys shook her head. "It was an agony to watch, to know you couldn't do one single thing about it."

Mel took the few steps that separated them, reached out, put her hand on Crys's bare arm, and rubbed the soft skin. But Crys gave no indication she was aware of Mel's touch.

"Diane was determined to fight it, and she did. To

her last breath. She put up an incredible battle, and at the end she didn't know how to stop fighting. She couldn't give in." Crys turned to look at Mel, remembered anguish reflected in her eyes.

"At the end I wanted to put my arms around her, hold her, tell her it was all too painful for her, tell her it was all right to let go. But I loved her and didn't want to lose her. I was a coward, Mel. I couldn't say it."

Tears welled in Crys's dark eyes, rolled down her cheeks, and Mel slid her arms around the other woman. She nestled Crys's head on her shoulder and held her close as she cried, her hand gently rubbing Crys consolingly on the back.

After some time Crys's sobs abated. "I'm sorry. I didn't mean to put all that on you, Mel," she said softly and moved back a little, Mel's arms still around her.

Slowly Mel released her, and Crys fumbled for a tissue in the pocket of her shirt and blew her nose. "I haven't cried like that in ages."

"It's all right, Crys." Mel couldn't seem to find anywhere to put her hands. She shoved them into the pockets of her jeans. "Don't they say it's healing to let it out rather than bottle it up inside?"

"I suppose so." Crys sniffed. "Plays havoc with the sinuses, though." She made an attempt at a laugh and then sighed.

"You must miss her very much," Mel said compassionately.

"Yes. I do." Crys looked up, and her gaze met Mel's, held that gaze for long moments.

And then the quality of the atmosphere began to

change. The air about them seemed to come alive, seemed to expand with glowing shards of electricity.

Mel's mouth was suddenly dry. She felt hot and then cold and she ached to take Crys in her arms and place burning kisses on the curve of smooth flesh where Crys's shoulder joined her neck. And her tongue tip unconsciously dampened her parched lips.

Crys's gaze was still locked with Mel's, her dark eyes burnished bright, and Mel heard her catch her breath.

CHAPTER SEVEN

Then Mel reached out, gently cupped the side of Crys's face with the palm of her hand, and let the pad of her thumb slide slowly over Crys's still damp cheek. She leaned forward, rested her other hand on the swell of Crys's hip as she lowered her head and put her lips to that so inviting curve below Crys's ear, her tongue at last tasting the warm flesh.

Crys groaned slightly, and Mel felt Crys's breath feather her earlobe. A heady surge of desire swelled instantly inside Mel, and she leaned into Crys, felt the exquisite softness of her breasts, her stomach, her thighs making delicious contact with her own.

Mel's lips slid along the smooth curve of Crys's cheek, touched her lips, drew back, touched again, her tongue tip now seeking the softness within. And Crys opened her mouth and hungrily kissed Mel back.

Mel trembled. She gave a soft groan of wanting, moving with unconscious sensuality, straining against Crys's body.

Suddenly Crys stiffened and pulled back so that she could look into Mel's eyes. Mel went to draw Crys back into her arms, but Crys frowned, whimpering softly.

"No, Mel. Please. We shouldn't be . . . we can't . . . I . . ." And Crys was moving away, putting cold distance between them.

Mel had a blinding flash of déjà vu. This couldn't be happening again. "Crys, please. Don't go. I didn't mean to —"

Crys stopped and turned back to Mel. "I know you didn't. It was my fault. I shouldn't have —"

"It wasn't anybody's fault," Mel began.

"Perhaps not. Maybe *fault* wasn't exactly the word." Crys swallowed, and Mel's eyes focused on the still erratic beating of the pulse at the base of her throat. "Look, Mel. I don't want to take advantage of you at the moment. We've been spending a lot of time together, and you're vulnerable just now. You've recently broken up with your boyfriend and —"

"You think I'm pining for Terry? Do you think that's what this is about?" Mel asked, dismay mixed with angry disbelief.

"Well, it's very emotionally upsetting and —"

"And don't forget the sex," Mel put in bitterly.

"The . . . I . . ." Crys swallowed again. "I didn't say —"

"But that's what you meant." Mel suspected she was being unreasonable, but she couldn't seem to stop herself. "You think I'm missing sex so much I'd take it anywhere I can get it. Even with a woman?"

Crys paled, flinching as though Mel had slapped her. She drew a deep breath. "I didn't say that," she stated, clipping her words.

"Maybe it's true," Mel said flatly, and Crys's features hardened.

"I'm going to bed now, Mel," she said levelly. "We've had a heavy day, and we're both tired. And I think we've both said more than we should have."

"I haven't," Mel said defiantly. "I haven't said nearly enough." She took a step toward Crys, and the other woman moved backward, clasping the chair behind her for support.

"I don't think it's wise for us to discuss this now," Crys said quickly.

Mel sighed and turned away, all of the fight suddenly going out of her. Was she a masochist? Crys wasn't interested in her. She'd made it perfectly plain all those years ago. So why was Mel pushing the point? It was futile, and it could only mean more grief for her.

Tonight, those few precious moments when Crys had kissed Mel back had been a purely physical response on Crys's part. And Mel didn't much care for the sudden thought that she may have taken advantage of Crys's moment of weakness. Perhaps it was as well that Crys had come to her senses and called a halt before more damage to their friendship had been done.

"Maybe you're right," Mel said with all the composure she could muster. "Go on to bed, Crys."

"Mel, I, I do think it would be best if we sorted this all out in the morning, when we've had time to put some space between us. Will you . . ." Crys paused. "Will you be all right?"

Mel nodded tiredly and walked toward her room, passing Crys as she still stood stiffly, her hand on the lounge chair. At the door Mel stopped and looked back at Crys.

"And just for the record, it wasn't just sex. Not tonight," she said flatly and continued out into the hallway. "And not the last time."

Crys sat down at her silky oak dressing table and regarded herself critically in the oval mirror. She looked exactly what she was, she decided, a forty-two-year-old woman who had had a very bad night's sleep. What little sleep she had had, that was. Damn Mel!

Crys sighed. No, it wasn't Mel's fault that Crys had slept badly. It was her own. She'd brought it all on herself by allowing Angela to talk her into having Mel down here to stay.

She should have known what would happen, she told herself disparagingly. The warning signs had been there over ten years ago, and they still held good. Mel was . . .

Crys absently ran her brush through her hair. Mel was exactly what she'd always been. A warm, loving child who had grown into a wonderfully caring, loving adult. That hadn't changed.

And, Crys admitted painfully to herself, neither had the attraction between them. It still lay dormant so very close to the surface, as it had all those years ago.

It was the timing that had been wrong, Crys reflected. First it was their ages. Then it was the disastrous circumstances of Crys's mixed-up life.

After Paul had won custody of their son, Crys had thought she'd lose her sanity. She sank deeper and deeper into a gray depression, one she had to drag herself out of for David's weekly visits.

Diane was pressuring Crys to move in with her and Crys knew how Paul would react if he found out she was living with Diane. Crys felt Paul was pulling her one way and Diane was pulling her another. And David was the vulnerable child caught right in the middle.

Crys knew she owed Diane some support as she'd just lost her teaching job, but Crys's contact with her son had been at stake. She'd needed Diane to understand that. The result was that Crys's relationship with Diane had been wavering on very shaky ground. It had all been so harrowing.

And in the middle of it had been Mel, who had suddenly become transformed from a gangling child into a very attractive, though very young, woman. Crys had to continually remind herself that Mel was, in all essence, still an uncertain teenager, one who was perhaps a little less worldly than other young women her age.

Mel continued to confide in Crys just as she'd always done and, in the midst of her own anxiety, Crys had tried to remain constantly available to the young girl. Mel was always at loggerheads with her mother, and Crys continued to be the go-between, the mediator.

When Mel admitted she didn't want to go to the high school formal dance, which was something of a tradition in the final year of secondary school, Angela had been disbelieving and then frankly impatient with her younger daughter. Angela couldn't understand how Mel was so different from her older sister. Amber had shone at her own formal dance.

Crys had always known that when it came to her two daughters, Angela's usual astuteness and practical common sense went completely out the window. Angela could not comprehend that Mel and Amber were totally different personalities and that while Amber was a carbon copy of her mother, Mel was just the opposite.

So when Mel continued to insist she didn't want to attend the dance, Crys had tactfully intervened on Mel's behalf, diplomatically trying to make Angela understand that Mel might not be ready for the social interaction of adolescence.

That was ridiculous, Angela had retorted. Of course Mel would go to the dance. And she'd remained adamant, until eventually Mel had caved in under the pressure and gone to the dance with the nice-looking boy who lived around the corner.

Mel hadn't said much about the dance itself, but a

week later she'd gone to the movies with the same young man. Angela had airily said to Crys, *I told you so.*

One afternoon after school, not long after Mel started dating Gary, Mel had stopped by to chat with Crys as she usually did. That particular afternoon Crys could tell that Mel was obviously concerned about something and wanted to talk about it. They'd sat down at the dining room table, and Crys had handed Mel a cold soft drink while Crys poured herself a cup of coffee.

For a while they discussed how they'd spent their respective days, and then Crys had gently inquired after Mel's young man. Mel gazed morosely at her Coke and shrugged her indifference.

"I guess Gary's all right as guys go," she said, and then she'd grimaced. "But he's so intense. He tried to kiss me the other night."

"That's kind of the way it usually goes," Crys replied lightly.

Her mind threw up an imagined scenario where the young man in question pulled Mel into a rough and inexperienced embrace and kissed her urgently. Crys thought she'd find it amusing, but just as suddenly she found she didn't particularly want to go into details of this aspect of Mel's life, and especially not with Mel herself.

"Am I expected to enjoy it, Crys?" Mel was asking, and Crys tried to pull herself together.

"Expected? Well, I don't know that great expectations are set in stone. I guess it all depends on who's doing the kissing," she said carefully, and Mel frowned.

"Well, I didn't enjoy it," she exclaimed. "Good

grief! I felt like he was going to suck me down whole and he'd end up like a python with a chicken in its stomach only I'd be the chicken and he'd slowly digest me."

Crys did laugh then. "Doesn't present the best of pictures, Mel."

Mel grinned reluctantly. "I was using poetic license. But seriously, Crys," she continued, undaunted. "I don't like all this dating and stuff. I wish Mum wouldn't push me to do it. And I don't care if Amber has millions of boyfriends and loves going out. I'd rather be at home with —" Mel paused and looked down at the table, her finger rubbing at the ring of condensation left by her cold soda can. "I'd rather be at home with you guys," she finished.

"You don't have to keep going out with Gary just to please your mother if you don't like him," Crys said, hoping Angela wouldn't be annoyed with her for siding with Mel. But Mel was obviously unhappy about it all. It seemed pointless to Crys to force her into something she wasn't ready for.

"It's not Gary exactly," Mel conceded. "I mean, it's okay when we go out in a group. But when we're on our own I, well, I hate trying to make conversation. And I really hate waiting for him to get up the courage to put his arm around me. And I'd rather he didn't, anyway. It's, well, humiliating."

Crys sighed. "I know, Mel. But it will get easier," she said sympathetically.

Mel stood up and walked across to gaze up at the painting Crys had on the wall. She took a sip of her Coke. "Did it get easier for you?"

Crys tensed uneasily. "I guess so. Yes."

"Did you go out with other guys besides Paul?"

Mel asked, still not looking at Crys, and Crys hesitated.

"No," she said at last. "No, I didn't. Paul was the first."

"Did you sleep with him before you got married?"

Crys stood up too. "Mel, I don't see — Has Gary been pressuring you to have sex with him?"

"No." Mel denied quickly and turned to face Crys. "I know he wants to, but I don't think he's game. He just, you know, touches me. I don't, well, you know —" Mel exhaled loudly.

Crys took a calming breath. "Mel, you don't have to do anything with Gary, with anyone, that doesn't feel right for you. You don't have to . . . You see, sleeping with someone, it's not just the physical side of it. You have to consider the emotional relationship and all that comes with it and —" Crys stopped and raised her hands helplessly and let them fall. "Look, Mel. I really think you should be talking to your mother about this."

"Are you kidding?" Mel rolled her eyes toward the ceiling. "Mum would freak out."

"I'm sure she wouldn't." Crys hoped this would be the case.

Mel turned back to gaze at Crys's painting, her hands worrying at the aluminum can she held. "When did you know you were a . . . that you liked women?"

Crys leaned against the dining room table for support. This conversation had taken a turn into previously uncharted waters, and Crys wasn't certain in which direction it was heading. Although she had heavy misgivings that she might. She desperately hoped not.

Suddenly she didn't know if she was capable of discussing this specific subject with Mel. Somehow, she'd have to head Mel off onto safer conversational ground. "I, well, I suppose, deep down, I always knew I preferred women. But . . ."

"And when you went out with Paul," Mel continued in a rush, "did you feel . . . did you wish he was a girl?"

"It didn't, I mean, it wasn't quite like that." How had it been? she asked herself. If she was honest she'd say that every time Paul kissed her she'd wanted it to be Diane. But she couldn't tell Mel that.

Crys pushed herself away from the table, resolutely straightening her spine. "Mel, I don't want to talk about this just now."

"Why not?" Mel had turned from the painting again and walked a few steps closer to Crys. "If you knew you were gay, why did you go out with Paul? Did you feel you had to?"

Crys swallowed. "Something like that."

The air in the room seemed suddenly thick with an inexplicable tension, and Crys felt hot and ill at ease.

"I don't want to go out with Gary," Mel said softly, her voice slightly husky.

"All right." Crys tried to relax her tensed muscles. "That's okay. Just tell him so next time he asks you."

"I sort of did."

"You did?" Crys made herself smile. "Well, that's fine then."

Mel's gaze met Crys's, and something in the young girl's expression had Crys's heart beating a wild tattoo in her chest. She swallowed convulsively again.

"There's plenty of time for you to meet another young man, one you do like. Someone special," she said, giving a small cough as her throat seemed to close on her.

"I already have," Mel said levelly. "I mean, there is someone I really like. Someone special."

Crys folded her arms casually across her chest and conjured up another smile. "There is? So what's he like? Do we know him?"

"No." Crys watched a pulse throbbing in Mel's throat. "It's" — she swallowed nervously — "it's not a guy."

Crys didn't know what to say. It hadn't come as a surprise, but hearing Mel actually put it into words ... Crys stood there transfixed and watched as Mel took a couple of hesitant steps across the room until she stood in front of Crys.

She's grown so tall, Crys thought illogically, and then Mel leaned forward and put her lips on Crys's.

It was a soft, quick kiss, and Mel pulled back a little, looking into Crys's startled eyes.

"I've wanted to do that for such a long time," she said hoarsely and moved closer, kissing Crys again, this time with more confidence.

The softness of Mel's mouth was velvety, her tongue tasting of Coca-Cola as she slipped it between Crys's lips. A fire of pure desire ignited inside Crys, raged to engulf her, and for wild, erotic seconds she responded, returning Mel's impassioned kiss.

Then Crys came excruciatingly to her senses. She was horrified at herself as she thrust Mel away from her. "No! Mel, stop. We, you, we can't do this."

Mel's face had paled. "I love you, Crys," she said brokenly. "I have for ages."

Crys moved away, raking her hand agitatedly through her hair. "I, Mel, you don't know what you're saying."

"I do know what I'm saying," Mel cried fervently. "And I know how I feel."

"No, you don't." Crys held up her hand, and part of her noticed her hand was shaking. "Please. We have to stop this now. I can't. It's all too much for me. I mean, your mother —" She shook her head and looked at Mel, desperately trying to find the right words to explain why this was totally impossible.

Mel's young face was stricken, and she put one hand to her mouth. Before Crys could stop her, she'd turned and run out of the house.

Crys sighed. She wasn't proud of her behavior with Mel all those years ago. Although she'd followed Mel, tried to explain, to make amends for her rejection, she suspected she'd failed miserably at the time. Mel had certainly avoided her afterward, and who could blame her? And at the time Crys admitted she'd taken the easy way out, deciding to leave things as they were, that it was probably for the best anyway.

Yet only she knew how much she'd missed Mel's smiling face and dry humor. Or that deep inside her she'd carried that burden of guilt.

She'd felt conscience-stricken because in those few moments back then she knew she'd responded to Mel's fervent kiss in a way she'd never reacted to anyone else. Not even Diane. So it was hardly Mel's fault that she had misinterpreted Crys's response, for Crys had certainly not repulsed the young girl. She'd kissed Mel back, and she knew she shouldn't have.

What a disaster it had been. And last night she had almost repeated it. There was a lot of truth in the old saying that there was no fool like an old fool. That said it all. She was an old fool.

Crys sighed again and glanced at her wristwatch. Well, there was nothing to be gained by skulking in her room. She had work to do, and she had to face Mel sometime. She'd simply tell Mel she was sorry and that she'd already forgotten the incident. They would just go on as before.

Go on as before? Crys groaned softly. What a bitter joke that was. If only . . .

Determinedly Crys stood up. Yet all she wanted to do was crawl back into bed. Preferably with Mel, suggested that small, irrepressible part inside her, and she grimaced. *Cowardly* and *self-delusional* were only two of the disparaging adjectives that came to her mind to describe herself as she opened the door and left her room, heading along the hallway.

The smell of perking coffee wafted from the kitchen, so Crys surmised Mel wasn't languishing in her own bed. *Well, here goes nothing,* she said to herself as she continued on her way.

Crys entered the kitchen and paused as she saw Mel standing in profile, her tall body leaning with one hip resting against the sink. Crys was sure her heart lurched physically in her breast, and she swallowed quickly. Unaware of Crys's presence, Mel was gazing out through the kitchen window, slowly sipping her cup of coffee.

Only then did Crys recall Mel's parting words of the evening before. It wasn't just sex, she'd said.

CHAPTER EIGHT

Mel had slept rather badly and was wide awake as dawn lightened the sky. Her mind kept playing over the scene with Crys the evening before. The searing heat of desire, the cold anguish of rejection. And her foolishness at allowing herself to be caught in a replay of her humiliation as a teenager, and with the very same woman.

She knew she should simply pack up and leave. That would sort out the entire fiasco. She should take herself out of Crys's life and save them both any on-going embarrassment.

The last time it had happened it had been Crys who had removed herself from Mel's life, first emotionally, although Mel conceded that had been her own fault for rashly kissing Crys. And then Crys had separated them physically when she bought the farm and moved here with Diane. Now it was only fair that Mel take her turn, she told herself bitterly.

She hugged her pillow as she recalled the absolute mortification she'd felt when she'd kissed Crys that first time and Crys had pushed her away. Mel had run then, home to a thankfully empty house. Her mother and sister were out somewhere, her stepfather still at work, and she'd reached the sanctuary of her room, closing the door on the outside world.

Totally devastated, she'd thought her life was over. Dry-eyed, she sat on her bed, her mind and body completely numb. Crys had been part of her life for so long, had come to mean so much to Mel, and now Mel had spoiled the special friendship they'd shared.

Why had she done it? What had possessed her to try to . . . ? Mel didn't even know what she'd wanted to eventuate. All she'd known was an urgent need to kiss Crys's full lips and dissolve into her body. She hadn't dared to really think past that.

Of course Crys had eventually followed her that day, although Mel couldn't have told if it was five minutes or five hours later.

Through the haze of remorse-filled agony, she had heard Crys call her name, was aware of her footsteps approaching along the hallway and of Crys's hesitant knock on the bedroom door.

Mel hadn't moved a muscle or spoken a word, and Crys had slowly opened the door and taken a step inside.

"Mel?"

Mel couldn't look at the other woman, let alone reply.

"Mel, I'm sorry," Crys said softly. "I shouldn't have . . . I didn't mean to, well, fob you off the way I did. It was such a . . . You took me by surprise, that's all. I just didn't know how you felt."

Mel clutched her hands together in her lap, her eyes focused on watching her knuckles turn white. Surprisingly, there was no pain. Not in her hands.

"Mel, please," Crys pleaded. "Please look at me."

Mel didn't, and then Crys sat down on the bed beside her, and Mel knew instinctively that Crys was being careful not to touch her.

"Just because you don't care much for dating at the moment doesn't mean you're . . . You're only sixteen, Mel, and —"

"I'll be seventeen in two weeks' time," Mel heard herself say petulantly.

"Yes, well." Mel heard Crys sigh. "Mel, interaction with young men is only part of your life, and it doesn't have to be the focus until you're ready for it to be. And you also get to decide just how much of a part it will be. But if you're not ready, that's fine. Forget about it for a while. You'll meet someone and you'll know —"

"Like you knew when you met Paul?" Mel asked scathingly, and she felt Crys stiffen beside her.

"I'm not such a good role model," she said flatly.

"I've made something of a mess of my life. And I wouldn't want to see you do that with yours."

"I love you, Crys," Mel said. Tears blurred her vision as Crys gently took her hand.

"I'm very flattered that you think you feel that way, Mel," she said carefully. "And I know that at the moment you think —" Crys sighed again. "Mel, it's okay for you to have a, well, a crush, if you like, on someone older, someone you think you admire. That's all part of growing up. But it will pass. Things will sort themselves out."

Mel deliberately removed her hand from Crys's. "You mean I'll turn un-gay?"

"No, I didn't mean that. It has nothing to do with being straight or gay. But if you do genuinely feel you might be a lesbian, there are people far more qualified than I am that you can talk to. And you can talk to them quite anonymously on the telephone. That could help."

"What will they do? Introduce me to other young people my own age who think they might be gay too?" Mel asked scornfully.

"Perhaps."

Mel looked sideways at Crys then. "I'm not interested in other young gay people. I'm interested in you."

Crys stood up, paced across the room, and turned back to face Mel. "Look, Mel. You know things have been pretty stressful for me this past year, with the divorce, the custody case. And you must know about Diane."

Mel thought she'd be unable to draw another

breath. Her throat ached with unshed tears. Of course she'd heard of Diane King. Who wouldn't have, with the publicity the Hewitts' court case had had. But Mel had never met the woman, had never seen her with Crys.

Mel swallowed painfully. She'd almost convinced herself that Diane was just a friend of Crys's. But hearing Crys mention her, say her name, brought reality back to earth with an almighty thud.

"Do you love her?" Mel asked, wanting and not wanting to hear Crys's answer.

"Yes. Yes, I do."

Crys's words were like a knife twisting inside Mel's breast.

"Diane and I, we've known each other and cared about each other for a long time."

Mel's gaze fell to her hands again, and Crys paused.

"Mel, look at me."

Mel looked up, wanting to lose herself in Crys's dark eyes, wishing they could both be transported somewhere far away from this place, from Diane King.

"I love you, too, Mel. But not the way I love Diane. Can you understand what I'm saying?"

Mel tore her gaze from Crys. She felt as though her heart was breaking.

"Mel? Please say you understand."

"Yes, I understand," Mel said flatly at last and she heard Crys exhale the breath she must have been holding.

"Good. Now we'll just put what happened this afternoon out of our minds."

"And forget it ever happened," added Mel evenly.

"Yes. I think it would be best. Don't you, Mel?"

"I guess so."

After a long moment Crys walked over to the door. "Just give it some time, Mel. As I said before, it will all sort itself out. Okay?"

Mel nodded forlornly.

"Well, I'd better go. Your mother will be home soon."

Crys had gone then, and that's when Mel had fallen back on her bed and cried.

And Mel had wanted to do just that last night after she'd left Crys. But she hadn't allowed herself that luxury. She'd cried enough tears in the last six months. Instead she'd got burningly angry with herself, chastised herself for putting herself, and Crys, into the same distressful position as she had all those years ago.

In the early hours of the morning, for what seemed like the hundredth time, her memory had tossed up the whole scene from over a decade ago, followed by the one last night.

And then suddenly had come that unnerving question. If Crys didn't care for her, why had Crys returned Mel's kiss when Mel had kissed her the first time, just as she had last night? Because Mel knew that on both occasions Crys hadn't been immediately repulsed. She *had* responded.

Now, over ten years later, Mel was no longer the naive teenager she'd been back then. She had the experience to recognize what had occurred. Crys had kissed her back, and her response hadn't been perfunctory. What if Crys *was* attracted to her?

Mel's stomach tensed, and she felt a spark of fire surge within her. She clenched her thighs together as she felt the blossom of an electrifying craving center between her legs. Last night Crys had also returned Mel's kiss, and for those few heady moments Mel had thought she'd faint dead away with wanting the other woman, with the wonder of having Crys in her arms.

It's purely physical, she told herself again, the thought surfacing to mercilessly taunt her. Crys had been on her own for five years, and Mel had been celibate for six months. Mel paused. Well, for a long time before that. She and Terry hadn't made love in months before Terry finally told Mel it was over. Was it just a physical reaction on both their parts?

Then it had occurred to Mel that she didn't know if Crys *had* been alone since Diane passed away. For all Mel knew Crys might already be in a relationship. There could be any number of reasons why she and another woman just didn't share the same house. Maybe Crys was involved with one of the women she went to dinner with on her Tuesday evenings out. Mel tortured herself with this possibility, recoiling from the picture of Crys making love to another woman. Mel shifted uneasily, hurriedly banishing that thought to the back of her mind.

Last night probably was simply a moment of weakness, hers and Crys's. And if they recognized that then maybe they could put it behind them. *Or maybe they should just go to bed together and get it over with,* said a wicked voice inside Mel. Then they could put that behind them, too.

Irritatedly Mel flung herself out of bed. She couldn't bear it a moment longer, wallowing and churning over what might or might not have happened or what might or might not happen in the future. Apart from that, lying in bed was far too conducive to thinking about Crys and, moments of weakness or not, Mel knew she still wanted the other woman, wanted to feel Crys's arms around her again, wanted to take her to bed, to make love to her forever.

Mel could hear no movement from Crys's bedroom, so she forced herself to leave her room and went tentatively into the kitchen, but Crys wasn't there either. With a small sigh of relief Mel busied herself going through the motions of putting on the coffee and dicing some fruit. Crys liked fresh fruit with her cereal. She set the table and poured herself a cup of coffee.

She gazed out the window at the beauty of the dew-damp green lawn, the trees, the clear morning sky. This was a beautiful place, and she'd grown to love the peacefulness, the calmness it engendered.

But what if Crys asked her to leave? Would Crys do that? Mel had to admit it could happen. And what would she do if Crys *did* want her to go? She realized now just how much she wanted to stay.

With a sinking feeling, Mel realized she hadn't exactly been gracious when Crys drew a halt to their embrace. In fact, she'd been quite cutting, asking Crys if she thought Mel was so desperate for sex she'd even take it with a woman.

Mel suddenly realized what she'd said, and she cringed. What had possessed her to say that? It would have sounded to Crys like — Oh, no. What else could Crys have thought Mel was implying? Only that she, Mel, was straight. There would be no reason why Crys would think any differently. She would also be under the misapprehension that Terry had been a man, just as Mel's mother was.

Mel took another sip of her coffee. She'd have to try to find some way to tell Crys the truth. Her mother as well. It had all become so complicated, and a small lie by omission had become a fully fledged web of deceit.

Sighing dejectedly, Mel turned slightly, and there, standing in the kitchen doorway, was Crys.

"Good morning. You're up early," Crys said evenly enough, although to the supersensitive Mel she sounded a little wary.

"Yes. I thought I might as well start breakfast."

There was a moment of unsettled silence.

"Shall I pour your coffee?" Mel put in quickly and Crys nodded, moving into the room.

"Thanks." Crys sat down at the small table, and Mel carefully set Crys's cup of coffee by her plate of cereal and fruit. "Thanks for this, too." Crys indicated the food in front of her.

"That's okay." Mel sat down in her chair. She felt compelled to look across at Crys. "I woke up early."

Their gazes met, skittered away, and then Crys sighed.

"Mel, about last night. I think I should apologize."

"You don't have to. It's okay," Mel said quickly. "Forget about it. I already have." *What a mammoth fib that was,* she accused herself, and glanced across at Crys again.

Crys's expression was unreadable. She absently spooned some sugar into her coffee. "I don't want us to feel uncomfortable with each other," she said carefully. "Maybe we should talk about it. Clear the air."

Mel swallowed. And suddenly she wanted to shout at Crys to stop. She felt like a gauche teenager, and she didn't want to hear Crys say it all over again, that she was flattered, that she loved Mel, but not in *that* way.

Because, regardless of the past and adolescent crushes, Mel was beginning to suspect she was way past all that, that she was well on the way to loving Crys in exactly *that* very way. And Crys simply wasn't interested.

"It doesn't matter, Crys," she said as evenly as she could. "We were both tired. You were upset. I just meant to, you know, comfort you."

Crys deliberately stirred her coffee. "I see. Well then, perhaps you're right. If you're sure, we'll just forget it."

"Yes."

Crys looked across at Mel, and something flickered briefly in her eyes, a flash of emotion Mel was almost sure was regret. Mel's nerve endings sprang to attention. Had Crys wanted to . . . ? What if Crys . . . ? Mel's mouth went dry.

Maybe Mel should tell Crys the truth now. Well, part of it, the part about Terry anyway, sort out that particular misconception. She was trying to decide just how to bring the topic into the conversation when the telephone jangled and they both literally jumped at the sound.

Mel was the first to recover, and she reached out to take the receiver from the kitchen extension on the wall.

"Hello. Mel speaking," she said a little breathily.

There was a moment of silence that echoed down the phone line.

"Hi, babe. How are you?"

Mel's fingers fumbled and she almost dropped the phone. "Who . . . ? What . . . ?" But Mel recognized the voice immediately.

CHAPTER NINE

"Don't tell me you've forgotten me so soon, babe?" Terry's familiar voice held a note of teasing, and Mel knew the other woman was smiling.

"Oh. Hi." Mel swallowed. "I, how are you?"

"Comme ci comme ça. You know how it is." Terry paused. "I've missed you, babe," she added, her voice low.

"You have?" Mel said stiltedly, so aware of Crys sitting opposite her. Would Crys be able to hear Terry's voice?

"Of course I've missed you. I wish you'd stayed here in Melbourne. When are you coming home?"

Mel pulled herself together. How dare Terry ask that when she was the one who had been responsible for Mel leaving? "I'm not, Terry," she said levelly. "I can't imagine why you'd think I would be."

There was the sound of Crys's chair moving, and Mel looked across to see Crys getting to her feet. She mimed to Mel that she was going over to the shed. And Mel could only watch impotently as Crys turned and left Mel alone with her phone call.

"Why wouldn't I? I do miss you, babe."

"Oh, sure." Mel changed hands, her arm stiff where she'd tensed at the sound of Terry's voice. "And stop calling me that, Terry. You know I never liked it."

"Never?" Terry laughed softly. "I distinctly remember you used to go crazy when I whispered that in your ear when we made love."

"Where's what's-her-name?" Mel asked deliberately, and she heard Terry sigh.

"Maureen and I decided we'd go our separate ways."

"I see." Mel realized she was totally unmoved by this revelation. "How did you find me, Terry?" she asked and Terry gave a soft laugh.

"It sure wasn't easy. I eventually got onto your sister, and she gave me your number. She told me you were staying on a farm, of all things." Terry laughed again. "I somehow can't imagine you down on the farm."

"Amber gave you my number?"

"Sure. Why wouldn't she give your number to your writing partner, Marie-Therese? So, what's the story with this farm you're staying at? Is it some health farm or something? Because, believe me, babe, you don't need to do anything to that beautiful body of yours."

"It's not a health farm. It's" — Mel paused — "just a farm. But Crys grows different types of wild food."

"Cris?" Terry picked up on the name. "As in Christine or Christopher?"

"Does it matter?" Mel searched frantically for something to say to change the subject, but her brain seemed to be working at half pace.

"Hang on a minute," Terry was saying. "Now I get it. Your sister said you were staying with a friend of your mother's. Cris? Isn't that the woman you had the hots for when you were a kid?"

Mel glanced guiltily around to make sure Crys hadn't returned. She knew what Terry was like. Mel would have to tread carefully or Terry wouldn't let the subject go. "As a matter of fact, Crys was our next-door neighbor in Brisbane. I'm helping her out for a few weeks."

There was another short silence. "So are you picking up where you left off? Making up for lost time."

"Terry, you're being ridiculous."

"She must be getting a bit long in the tooth if she's your mother's age," Terry continued. "Not that hard up, are you, babe?"

Mel bit back an angry retort. If she protested too much, she knew Terry was more than capable of

123

reading between the lines. "Crys is a family friend. That's all. So what are you ringing me about anyway?"

"Sounds as if you're still brassed off with me. Are you, Mel?"

"What do you think, Terry?" Mel said sarcastically. "That I'd see having someone I loved betray me as simply being an exercise in character building?"

"I guess I deserve that." Terry sighed. "And I'm sorry things turned out the way they did."

"I'm sure you are." Mel bit out the words tersely.

"I am. Really. And I wanted to talk to you, hear your voice. Can't I ring you and tell you I miss you?" Terry's own voice had dropped cajolingly again. "Aren't you glad I miss you, lover?"

"Terry, please!"

"Okay. I'm sorry, Mel. Maybe a long-distance phone call isn't the right way to be discussing this."

Mel took a deep steadying breath. "Stop playing games, Terry. What do you really want?"

Terry sighed exaggeratedly. "All right. But I did want to talk to you, too. Actually, I've finished the book and I wanted to get it to you. I told Tommy you'd have the illustrations done as soon as possible. We are under contract, so if I express post the manuscript up to you do you think you can get them done within a couple of weeks?"

"A couple of weeks?" Mel exclaimed. "We haven't even discussed the story."

"Well, I didn't know where you were. It's no big deal, Mel. I used the characters from the last book. We were going to do a story about Wendy the Wombat, remember? Well, this is it. What do you say,

Mel? I mean, we're professionals, aren't we? We should be able to work together regardless."

Mel sighed. "Did you tell our editor that we'd split?"

Mel heard Terry pause and knew the answer before the other woman spoke.

"The subject didn't come up. All Tommy's interested in is the final product."

Mel suspected that was true, and she sighed. "All right. I'll get the illustrations done. When you send the manuscript you'd better add any ideas you have."

"Oh, I'm full of ideas. You know that," Terry murmured.

Mel felt like slamming the phone down and to hell with the book. But as Terry said, they did have a contract and it had to be honored.

"You know what I mean," Mel said wearily.

"So where shall I send it?" Terry asked, and Mel gave her the address.

"Okay. It'll be there tomorrow. Well, I guess I'd better go." Terry paused again. "Thanks, Mel. I'll be in touch, babe."

Mel set the phone back on the hook and sat staring at the remains of their breakfast. She'd just spoken to Terry. After six long months of silence. And Terry said she missed Mel, that her romance with Maureen was over. If this had happened any time in the previous six months Mel would have been over the moon. Wouldn't she?

She tried to analyze her feelings. She'd been surprised, shocked even, to hear Terry's voice. But that was all. No surge of excitement. No glow of pleasure. Mel quelled a spurt of guilt. After spending six years with someone she should feel more than that, shouldn't she?

If Terry walked in now, how would she react? Mel asked herself. She suspected she'd be simply annoyed. Did that make her superficial? Shallow? Or had she simply moved on, put Terry and her infidelity, her betrayal, behind her?

Mel stood up, made herself concentrate on clearing away the dishes. She'd almost finished when the phone rang again.

Mel paused. Surely Terry wouldn't ring back so soon. She picked up the receiver and hesitantly answered.

"Mel?" Amber's voice made Mel's tense muscles relax and she sat down.

"Oh. Hi, Sis!" she said thankfully. "How are you?"

"Fine. Apart from wanting to draw and quarter a couple of so-called tradesmen."

Mel laughed. "That sounds like the universal cry of the home builder."

"I guess. But I've told Adam he has to get serious with them. If they play this male buddy-buddy stuff much longer, we'll still be waiting for the house to be finished at Christmas." Amber sighed. "Enough of that, though. I just wanted to tell you that I gave Crys's number to Marie-Therese. She rang me last night looking for you. Was that okay?"

"Sure," Mel replied evenly. "As a matter of fact, I've just spoken to her. I forgot to let her know I was coming down here to Uki."

"That's okay then. And I suppose, knowing Mum, she had you whisked away before you could tell anyone."

"That about covers it." Mel laughed.

"And how are things going down there? Are you enjoying seeing Crys again and are you having a good time?"

"Yes to both. I really like it down here."

"I thought you would. You and Crys always got on well." Amber seemed to hesitate. "Is Crys with anyone at the moment?"

"No," Mel replied carefully. "I don't think so. Why?"

"Oh, no reason," Amber said offhandedly. "It's five years since Diane died. I just thought she may have met someone. But getting back to what I rang you about. I don't usually pass out phone numbers, but I thought you wouldn't mind if I gave it to Marie-Therese. She seemed very nice, Mel."

"Mmm," Mel murmured noncommittally. "She wanted to send me the next book to start working on. How are my nephew and niece?"

Amber waxed poetic about her offspring, and then they said good-bye.

So Amber had thought Terry sounded nice. Well, when Terry wanted anything she could be exceptionally nice.

Mel sighed. What was the point in being bitchy? Mel told herself she was over all that. She had to let it go.

Half an hour later Mel found Crys shoveling seed through a sieve. As she approached the other woman, her gaze irresistibly skimmed over the curve of Crys's bent back, the rounded swell of her buttocks, and Mel felt a tantalizing flutter of pleasure wash over her.

Crys moved, bending her back as she worked, and Mel's attention was drawn to the rounded fullness of Crys's right breast as it strained against her shirt. Mel's step faltered, her knees going weak as she knew an instantaneous, almost overwhelming urge to gently follow the line of those incredibly sensual curves with the palm of her hand.

She coughed slightly to clear her suddenly dry throat, and Crys straightened and turned to look across at Mel as she put down her shovel.

"I've brought you fresh coffee." Mel held out the mug, wondering how she hadn't dropped it in her agitation. "You didn't finish your other one." Somehow she got her legs moving and covered the space between herself and Crys.

Crys took the coffee and smiled. "Thanks." She took a sip. "Mmm. You *do* make a great cup of coffee," she said easily.

Mel smiled back. "Want me to do some shoveling for a while?"

"Sure." Crys set her coffee mug on a shelf. "And I'll do some sifting."

"That was Terry," Mel said before she realized she had said the words.

Crys paused. "So I heard." Crys changed her mind and picked up her coffee again. "Is everything all right?" she asked gently.

"All right? Oh. Yes. I was, well, just a bit surprised to get the call. It's been over six months." Mel bit her lip, trying to find the words to explain that Terry and Marie-Therese were one and the same.

"So what happened between you two?" Crys was looking into her coffee mug.

"Just the usual." Mel shrugged. "Another woman."

"I'm sorry. That's so painful," Crys said sympathetically. "You feel betrayed."

"Yes. That's exactly how I felt," Mel agreed. "I think that was what hurt the most. The subterfuge. The dishonesty of it all."

Crys nodded. "And are they still together, Terry and the other woman?" she asked evenly.

Mel shook her head. "Terry said they weren't. When it happened I couldn't see it lasting. I told Terry so at the time, but . . . Anyway, that's the way it goes."

Mel shoved her hands into her pockets. "Actually, it was Marie-Therese who wanted to get in touch with me. She's finished the book and is sending me the manuscript so I can do the illustrations," Mel said quickly. "Our editor wants them pretty much straightaway, so I'll have to get busy to have them finished in time."

"That's no problem, Mel. You know you don't have to work out here. Take as long as you like to do your illustrations."

"Thanks. It'll probably take me a couple of weeks. But I can help you when I'm taking a break."

"There's no need." Crys finished her coffee. "So Marie-Therese asked Terry to call you?" she said, not looking at Mel as she put her cup down.

"Um, no. Not exactly." Mel hesitated.

"Was Marie-Therese the other woman?" Crys asked, and Mel's jaw slackened in surprise.

"No, of course not. What made you think that?"

Crys shrugged. "Terry ringing you for Marie-Therese. And you don't talk about either of them very

129

much. I just put two and two together and thought I'd made four." She gave a crooked smile. "But I should have known, I never was very good at math."

"It was a young art student named Maureen. She took one of Terry's classes," Mel told her. At least that was true. "Well, guess I'd better get started or it'll be lunchtime before we know it."

Mel stretched and sat back from her work. She rubbed her eyes tiredly and glanced at the clock. Crys would be leaving in less than half an hour. Mel stood up and paced around the study.

Crys had asked Mel to go out to dinner with her and meet her friends, but Mel had declined, pleading the need to work.

Terry's manuscript had arrived the day after Mel spoke to her on the phone, and Mel had been working on the illustrations ever since. She'd stayed home working when Crys went to the market last weekend, although she had helped Crys load up the truck with her seedlings, her jams and jellies, and some potpourri Crys had been experimenting with, all to sell at her stall.

Now it was Tuesday, Crys's night to go out to dinner with her friends. Mel recalled her speculation that perhaps Crys was involved with one of the women she dined with on Tuesday evenings. If Mel accompanied Crys maybe she could put her theory to the test, see if there was someone else in Crys's life.

Mel shook her head. That was hardly a good reason to go out to dinner, she chastised herself. Of course, she could simply ask Crys if Crys had a partner. That would be the adult thing to do. Mel sighed, suspecting she didn't really want to know.

So why was she even considering going with Crys? Maybe she'd enjoy the interaction with other women, she told herself. She'd missed the regular socializing that had been part of her life in Melbourne, even though most of her friends had been Terry's friends too. That, of course, had made mixing with the usual crowd a little awkward at times, especially when Terry brought her new lover along.

Mel grimaced. No chance of old lovers here. Except Crys. And Crys could hardly be called a lover. Mel had loved Crys but, apart from that one kiss, well . . .

Sitting down again, Mel picked up her pencil, but she made no move to continue working. It seemed as though, as the saying went, her muse had gone. And sitting thinking about Crys and her maybe-lover was not going to have her muse rushing back.

Before she could change her mind, Mel packed everything up and went through to the lounge. Crys was watching the early edition of the news and she looked up as Mel entered the room.

"Sure the leftovers will be okay for your dinner?" Crys asked, muting the volume on the TV.

"Well, I was thinking perhaps I might change my mind. Maybe getting away for a few hours, a change of scene, might clear away the cobwebs. That's if the offer is still open," Mel added quickly.

"Of course it is." Crys smiled. "And I think a break will do you good. You've been working pretty full-on, so you must be exhausted."

"Just a bit stiff." Mel flexed her muscles unconsciously. "Have I got time for a quick shower?"

"Sure. No need to rush."

131

Mel showered quickly and hesitated over what she would wear. Crys was dressed casually but smartly, so Mel chose a pair of dark tailored slacks and then pulled on a pale green angora sweater. She ran a brush through her hair, grabbed her wallet and car keys, and joined Crys in the living room.

"That was quick." Crys stood up and flicked off the television set. "I was thinking if you don't want to, well, if you're too tired to want to bother with meeting new people we could always go somewhere else on our own for a meal."

Mel was tempted. Although it had nothing to do with being tired. The thought of dining alone with Crys, by candlelight, was more than a little enticing, but Mel wondered if it would be totally sensible on her part. It would only reawaken those heady feelings that she knew hovered so close to the surface. And she suspected she was far too tired to even try to fight them off.

"No, I'd really like to meet your friends," she said evenly. "As long as they don't mind me coming along with you."

Crys shook her head. "They won't. We try to keep these Tuesday evenings pretty flexible. Well, ready to go?"

"Shall I drive?" Mel held up her car keys. "Then you can relax and enjoy a glass or two of wine."

"What about you?"

Mel shrugged. "I'll stick to water tonight. If I have wine when I'm tired I'm almost instantly asleep."

After a short drive Mel parked the car and followed Crys into the restaurant. It was small and intimate, and a potbellied stove in one corner added a warm, cozy atmosphere. The owner greeted Crys by name and didn't hide her curiosity when she looked at Mel.

"Mel's the daughter of a friend of mine." Crys made the introductions. "Mel, this is Jo, a friend who owns this wonderful establishment."

"Well, me and the bank," laughed Jo and shook Mel's hand. "Nice to meet you, Mel."

Mel warmed to the woman's friendly face, knowing instinctively that Jo was a dyke.

"Go on through," added Jo. "Just about everyone's here, and I might even get a chance to join you all if it doesn't get too busy."

Crys led Mel out onto an enclosed side veranda. "Unless it gets really cold, we always eat out here. It's nice and private."

Half a dozen women were already seated around a long oval table, and they looked up with interest as Crys and Mel joined them.

"Did Crys say private? She means exclusive," laughed a dark-haired woman, dimples bracketing her laughing mouth.

"Margie is our comedian," Crys said as she and Mel sat down in the two remaining seats. Crys then proceeded to introduce everyone else. "Loretta. Billy. Sue. Josey. And?" Crys raised her eyebrows at the woman sitting beside Josey.

"Crys, this is Ingrid," Josey put in quickly.

Crys smiled at the woman. "Nice to meet you, Ingrid. Everyone, meet Mel Jamieson. Mel's my friend Angela's daughter."

"Don't worry, Mel. You don't have to remember who we are all at once," said Billy, who was obviously the oldest of the group.

"No. Ingrid is still trying to sort us out," Billy's

partner, Loretta, added easily. "You'll get the hang of us eventually."

"I'll do my best," Mel said with a grin. "And feel free to test me before we leave."

"Ah, to be young and have a retentive memory," sighed Loretta. They all groaned.

"Don't be fooled, Mel." Billy leaned forward. "This woman's memory is lethal. I can guarantee she never forgets a thing. Or lets me forget either."

There was much good-humored teasing, and then they all consulted their menus, everyone offering Mel recommendations.

The meal was delicious, and Mel relaxed, completely enjoying the company of Crys's friends. And yet she was still aware of Crys sitting beside her, her arm brushing Mel's as they ate, her knee so close beside Mel's.

Just before dessert arrived, Crys excused herself to go to the bathroom and Margie decided to go with her.

"Don't worry about Mel while you're away, Crys," said Billy with a wink at Crys. "We'll look after her. I can start by asking her about her etchings."

Mel laughed delightedly. "Now, etchings I can discuss till the cows come home."

She chatted with the other women, answering their interested questions about her experience in the publishing industry. Yet part of her was waiting for Crys to return. When Crys and Margie rejoined them, Mel glanced up and it seemed to Mel that Crys looked a little flushed.

Was Margie the woman Crys was involved with? Mel wondered. Then she reminded herself not to watch the interaction between the two women too closely in case Crys, or any of the others, noticed her interested regard.

Margie Donovan was perhaps a little older than Crys, her dark hair flecked with gray, but she seemed a very nice, outgoing person. It was certainly obvious that she and Crys were good friends. Mel's heart sank. Margie was also a very attractive woman and had obviously known Crys for some time. If Crys was involved with anyone in the group, Mel decided it had to be Margie.

"Crys says at the moment you're working on your next book," remarked Loretta, and Mel forced herself to concentrate on the conversation.

She told the women about Wendy the Wombat, and they all decided that the book sounded like a surefire bestseller.

"Did you hear they're having Roger Woodward at the music festival?" asked Sue, the quiet redhead. She turned to Mel. "Are you interested in music, Mel?"

"I like most types of music. Not too keen on jazz, though," Mel admitted.

"Nobody's perfect," said Billy with a mournful look. Loretta gave her a nudge.

"Don't give Mel a hard time, love. Everyone is entitled to her own likes and dislikes," she said and turned back to Mel. "Did Crys tell you about our local music festival?"

Mel shook her head.

"We have the Tyalgum Festival of Classical Music each year, and it's quite world-renowned."

Sue enthusiastically took up the story. "They have

outstanding performers and also focus on highlighting the talents of some of Australia's most successful young musicians."

"It was an amazing coincidence. You see, two musicians discovered by chance that the very unpretentious community hall has the most perfect acoustics you can imagine," continued Loretta. "Quite a phenomenon really. The festival's very popular with music lovers. It's on in a couple of months, and we all go every year. It's absolutely wonderful. You'll have to bring Mel along, Crys."

"I'd love to go," Mel said, and Crys nodded.

Eventually they called it a night and Mel drove them the short distance home. Once inside they walked along the hallway toward their rooms.

"Glad you enjoyed the evening," Crys said, stifling a yawn. "See you in the morning."

"I did enjoy it," Mel said honestly. "And Crys, I really liked your friends."

Crys smiled. "They liked you, too. Night, Mel." And then she was stepping into her room, closing the door behind her.

Crys wiped her hands distastefully on a piece of rag, grimacing at the grease and dirt smeared on her skin. The tractor was on its last legs, well, wheels, actually, she thought grimly. And she wondered for the umpteenth time why she was bothering to baby it into keeping going.

She knew she should trade it in on something more reliable, but she was disinclined to go into debt, not when she was just getting ahead. Maybe next year it would be different.

Crys poured herself a drink from her water bottle and leaned back against the tractor. From here she could see the study window. Mel would be working away on her illustrations. She was extremely talented, and Crys thought the work she'd already done was fantastic. No wonder she and Marie-Therese had done so well.

She smiled faintly, thinking back over her mistaken assumption that Mel's boyfriend had run off with her writing partner. It had seemed logical to Crys, allowing for the fact that Mel seemed at pains not to mention either of them. And no matter what Mel said, Crys suspected there was something amiss that Mel wasn't talking about.

Crys took a long, cool drink of water, and last night's dinner with her friends and Mel came into her mind. Mel had really enjoyed herself, seemed to relish the break from working. And she had fit in so well with everyone.

Crys smiled crookedly. Even Margie, who had apparently set herself the task of watching over Crys, had been captivated by Mel's easygoing nature.

When Margie had followed Crys to the bathroom, Crys had known she was in for an interrogation.

"Well! What a cutie!" Margie exclaimed when she and Crys were alone.

"I take it you aren't referring to me," Crys said dryly, and Margie rolled her eyes.

"You are too. But in this case I was meaning your young friend."

"Yes, Mel is nice. She was even likable as a teenager," Crys said carefully, making an effort to keep her tone light.

"Is she the one?" Margie asked, and Crys blinked in surprise.

"The one? I don't think I know what you mean."

Margie gave an exclamation of disgust. "Of course you don't."

Crys met Margie's gaze, but she was the first to look away. "She's Angela's daughter, Marg. I've known her since she was a kid."

"She's not a kid any longer, as I'm sure you've noticed," Margie stated blithely. "And she's also not exactly, unmoved, shall we say, by you."

"Unmoved?" Crys swallowed. "What do you mean?"

Margie laughed softly. "She's got it bad, love. Just like you have. Have you slept with her yet?"

"For heaven's sake, Marg. Of course I haven't. She's young enough to be my daughter."

Margie blew a disbelieving raspberry at Crys.

"And for your information," Crys continued, "she's straight."

Margie laughed mockingly. "Oh, Crys. Pull the other one. She's no more straight than I am."

CHAPTER TEN

Crys digested this comment and felt her pulse rate increase. "You don't know that, Margie."

"I'll bet my house on it. Trust me on this."

Crys took another steadying breath. "She's just broken up with her boyfriend of six years," she said with somewhat less conviction in her voice.

"We're all entitled to one mistake, love." Margie raised her eyebrows expressively. "I've even made that one myself."

"You have?" Crys looked at her friend in surprise. "You didn't tell me that."

"I was a mere child." Margie waved her hand in a dismissive gesture. "Fortunately it didn't take me long to realize what the problem was. No harm was done, and I moved on" — she winked at Crys — "to better things. So why can't Mel have done the same?"

Crys frowned and turned away to reach for a paper towel. "I'm attracted to her, Margie. I really am. And I don't know what on earth to do about it."

"You could start by kissing her."

"I didn't mean that literally." Crys crumpled the paper towel and tossed it into the bin.

"I know you didn't. I was just being my usual facetious self."

"You, facetious? I don't believe it," Crys said dryly. Margie gave her an old-fashioned look.

"How attracted to her are you? As in seriously attracted?" Margie asked, and Crys nodded unhappily. "Then let her know that. Kiss her, you fool."

"I already have kissed her," Crys admitted, feeling her face grow hot. "Twice."

"Twice? You have? Did she like it?"

"I think she did. I certainly did," Crys added with a grimace of self-derision. She folded her arms and leaned back against the wash basin. "Actually, she kissed me the first time. That was about eleven years ago."

"Eleven years!" Margie's mouth opened and closed for a moment before she pulled herself together. "She must have been —"

"Just seventeen," Crys finished for her. And then it was all coming out, including Crys's guilt over the way she'd handled the situation back then. "And when we kissed the other night I —" Crys swallowed. "I pushed her away again."

Margie's face was unsmiling as she listened to Crys's story. "You pushed her away? Good grief, Crys! Why? If you're attracted to her and everything, well" — Margie shrugged expressively — "What's the problem?"

"I thought she was . . . I didn't want to take advantage of her. She's vulnerable, just getting over a broken relationship."

"Console her," Margie said shortly.

"And she's Angela's daughter."

Margie pursed her lips as she considered that. "And I take it Angela doesn't know her daughter's a lesbian?"

"I don't know that either," Crys said unhappily. "Although I'm sure Angela would have said something if she did know."

"Well, I can see you wouldn't want to jeopardize your friendship with Angela, but if you do think this is the real thing, Crys, don't let the chance for happiness pass you by."

"Angela will love it if I —" Crys shook her head. "It doesn't bear thinking about."

"If Angela loves her daughter, she'll come around. She doesn't have a problem with you being a lesbian, does she?"

"No. But I'm not her daughter," Crys replied. "God, Marg! If Mel and I got together I have absolutely no idea how Angela would react."

Margie put her hand on Crys's arm. "When it really comes down to it, it's simply you and Mel. And after all you've been through, Crys, you deserve a little happiness for a change."

"I don't know about that, Margie. I didn't exactly

do the right thing when I took the easy way out with Mel all those years ago."

"That sounds like the old I-don't-deserve-to-be-happy syndrome. And what do you see as the right thing anyway, Crys? What more could you have done? When she told you she thought she was a lesbian you discussed it with her." Margie marked off the points on her fingers. "You made suggestions that she talk to a gay and lesbian info line. You didn't take advantage of her immaturity. And, let's face it, Crys. We'd all give our k. d. lang CDs to have a nubile young thing throw herself into our arms. Well," Margie grinned, "in our dreams."

"Right." Crys laughed too.

"But, seriously, Crys. Don't let Mel slip through your fingers if you think you two have got something going there. It's worth taking a chance or two, don't you think?"

Crys shrugged, unconvinced.

"Take some free advice from an old crone who's been there and done that before today. You know how long nights are when you're alone."

Crys looked at the other woman, and something in Margie's eyes made Crys pause. Crys had known Margie for years. She had been a friend of hers and Diane's. Did Margie mean . . . ?

And then Margie was laughing softly again. "Just exert your considerable and experienced charms and Mel will fall like a ton of bricks. She's more than halfway there now," she added as she opened the rest room door.

More than halfway there? Crys couldn't allow herself to even begin thinking Margie might be right.

If the kiss she and Mel had fleetingly shared the

other night was any indication . . . Crys's knees turned to water at the thought, and she quickly turned back to the tractor, fiercely concentrating on the job she was supposed to be doing.

A couple of days later Crys walked into the kitchen, stopping when she saw Mel pouring herself a cup of coffee.

Since her conversation with Margie, Crys had been careful to give Mel her space. With Mel working in the study and Crys outside, physically it had been easy. Emotionally Crys wasn't so sure.

"Taking a break?" she asked as Mel turned around.

"I thought I would. Oh, and Margie just rang."

"She did?" Crys frowned. "I didn't hear the phone."

"I was standing right beside it, so I probably picked it up before the buzzer rang in the shed." Mel took down another cup and poured a cup of coffee for Crys. "Margie said she's having a get-together tomorrow afternoon at her place. Some women are coming down from the Gold Coast for a car rally. They belong to a women's club. Feathers, I think she called it?"

Crys nodded.

"Anyway," Mel continued. "After the car rally they're going to end up at Margie's place for a swim and a barbecue. And Margie asked us to go."

"That was nice of her," Crys commented carefully.

"She said to be there about three-thirty or four." Mel took a sip of coffee. "Do you want to go?"

Crys paused. "I've got a lot to do tomorrow, and you're working hard on your illustrations."

"Actually, I'm doing quite well with them. I'm on the last one, and I'll be finished ahead of schedule so there's no worries there." Mel hesitated. "It might be fun."

"You want to go?"

Mel shrugged. "I enjoyed meeting your friends on Tuesday night, and Margie said they'd all be there."

"Well." Crys wavered. "If we're tired I guess we don't have to stay late."

The next afternoon Mel drove them over to Margie Donovan's small property at Tyalgum.

Margie's house was an attractive brick bungalow with wide wooden verandas. A landscaped courtyard led to a medium-sized pool.

When Crys and Mel arrived, women seemed to be everywhere, including a few swimming in the pool.

"Brrr!" Mel shivered. "They're swimming at this time of the day? It looks freezing. As we used to say in Queensland, they must be Victorians."

Crys laughed. "Margie has solar heating. Want to try it?"

"No, thanks," replied Mel. "I have thin tropical blood. I'll mill around the barbecue fire."

"Scaredy-cat." Crys teased softly as they joined everyone.

"Welcome!" Margie greeted them warmly. "I must say you two look happy and relaxed." She raised one dark eyebrow quizzically at Crys, and Mel was sure Crys flushed.

But then Billy and Loretta arrived, and the moment passed.

Billy set to cooking the steaks, and Mel helped Margie and Sue put the salads on the table for their buffet meal. Everyone sat around eating, laughing, and talking until night fell.

Margie lit some strategically placed braziers for light and warmth, for it was cooler now that the sun had set. She switched on her stereo and soon women were pairing off to dance on the veranda. Mel watched as Billy pulled Crys to her feet and swung her into a very invigorating jive. Mel got up with a group of women and threw herself into moving to the music.

After a while Margie hunted through her music collection, and a number of the visiting women entertained them with some lively line dancing. Mel and Crys allowed themselves to be talked into having a go, and with much hilarity they stumbled their way through a couple of the simpler dances.

"Wow! That was great, but exhausting," Mel said as she sat down beside Crys.

"You did really well," Crys complimented her. "Are you sure you haven't line-danced before?"

"No. I swear. I've always thought it was just country stuff. I didn't know it was so much fun." Mel smiled as she nibbled on some potato chips.

"Now for something slower for those of us who can't keep up the pace." Margie laughed as she changed the CD. She asked one of the women from the Gold Coast to dance, and they moved to the smoochie number.

Other couples joined them. Billy got up with Loretta, and before she realized what she was doing

Mel was taking Crys's hand, gently pulling her to her feet.

"Come on. This looks like a piece of cake after the line dancing." Mel slid her arms around Crys, and they moved together to the beat.

Mel lay in bed and tossed from side to side, the lyrics and tune of the last song she'd danced to with Crys sounding relentlessly in her head. She could feel Crys in her arms, Crys's warm breath on the side of her neck, Crys's breasts grazing, moving away, returning to touch her again.

They'd arrived home from Margie's barbecue and walked quietly toward their rooms. Mel could feel her heart pounding in her chest, and that same charged tension seemed to echo about them. Only tonight it had been unbelievably more compelling.

Mel paused, her hand on her doorknob. "Well, good night," she got out.

Crys's eyes seemed to sparkle in the artificial overhead hall light. "Yes. Good night, Mel."

Their eyes met, skidded away, then met again.

Crys's throat moved as she swallowed. "I'm glad we went. It was a lovely afternoon and evening."

Especially the evening, Mel wanted to say, but she just couldn't seem to force the words out. All she could manage was a nod.

Crys looked at her for long seconds, and then she moved on to her own room. "Sleep well," she said, and then she was gone.

And Mel could only make herself go through the motions of taking a shower and getting into bed.

Sleep well? If only . . .

The most sensible thing, she told herself what seemed like hours later, was to relieve all this pent-up tension in the most basic way, but somehow she knew that wouldn't help in the least. Momentarily maybe, but . . . Mel suspected she was way beyond that. She should have had a cold shower, she told herself irritatedly.

Glancing at the luminous dial on her bedside clock, she groaned. She was wide awake, and there was no way she was going to get any sleep in the foreseeable future.

Mel flicked on her reading lamp and threw back the covers. Shivering slightly, she slipped into a pair of warm track pants and pulled a sweater on over her short nightshirt. She sat back on the bed and thrust her bare feet into a pair of thick socks.

Then she switched out the light and felt her way into the hallway and on into the study, closing the door quietly behind her before flicking on the light. Crossing to her drawing board, she gazed critically at the mounted sketch.

She couldn't believe she'd accomplished so much in so short a time. It was just a little over a week since Terry's manuscript had arrived. Usually doing the illustrations took her weeks to complete. But then again, she couldn't say she'd worked on them so diligently before.

Terry had always subscribed to the all-work-and-no-play school of thought, and while Mel could see her point, she knew there had been times when Mel had simply wanted to closet herself in front of her drawing board and work. But Terry had usually coaxed her out to lunch, to a party, into the bedroom.

Mel sighed. Had she been so . . . she searched for the right word. *Pliant? Complacent?* It appeared that way from six months on.

Perhaps she had been too easily led by Terry, but she couldn't say she'd been all that unhappy. She and Terry had had their disagreements, and sometimes Mel knew she'd felt a little, well, uneasy. But most of the time she'd been quite satisfied with her life.

Yet this past week or so, working until her body ached, had filled her with a mixture of exhilaration and personal achievement that she hadn't felt before. And she knew what she'd completed was good. More than good. Maybe even the best she'd ever done.

She picked up her pencil. This one, of the chubby and appealing Wendy the Wombat inquisitively nosing her way into a box of magic tricks that were about to cascade all over the curious animal, would be ideal for the cover of the book.

Mel began to work. By the time she'd finished the illustration, her eyes were gritty and strained, her body stiff and tired. She stretched her muscles and gazed at the picture with satisfaction. Maybe a couple of finishing touches here and there on one or two of the others and she could get them off to Terry. Monday should see them ready to be sent away.

She cleaned up her workspace and then flicked off the light, waiting for her eyes to grow accustomed to the dark before opening the door. She went to return to her room, and then decided she needed a drink. In the kitchen she paused. Water or warm milk? Milk would be nice. Would Crys hear the microwave? Mel didn't think so.

Paddy and Misty materialized to wind themselves around Mel's ankles, mewing their starvation.

"Shh!" Mel admonished. "You can have a snack as long as you promise not to wake Crys."

Mel fetched their bowls and, in the light of the open refrigerator door, spooned some cat food onto the plates before taking them into the laundry, the cats following closely behind her.

Returning to the kitchen Mel poured a small glass of milk and placed it carefully in the microwave. She pushed the button and then flinched when the bell dinged as it had completed its cycle.

She would have liked to take the glass of warm milk back to bed with her but she suspected she'd probably spill it floundering around in the dark. She sipped the hot liquid, and her tummy rumbled, making her realize she was also suddenly hungry. She took a cookie from the jar and murmured appreciatively. Crys had always made the most divine chocolate chip cookies.

Mel swallowed the last of the milk and rinsed out her glass. Surrendering to temptation, she took another cookie with her as she moved back into the hallway, her hand running lightly along the wall to guide her.

She took a nibble of her cookie as she turned the knob to open her door. The cookie crumbled, and she made a grab for the falling fragments, biting off an exclamation of annoyance. Bending down she felt around for the errant cookie crumbs and almost overbalanced as a light came on under Crys's bedroom door.

As Mel started to rise, the door opened and Crys stood there, her body silhouetted by the bedside light.

"Mel?" she said, and then she saw Mel down on her haunches. She took a couple of steps into the hallway and stopped. "Mel? What's the matter? Are you all right?"

Mel pushed herself hurriedly to her feet. "I'm fine. I just dropped part of my cookie." She tried to laugh. "Caught having a midnight snack." She held up the remainder of the cookie.

"Oh. All right then."

They were mere feet away from each other, and suddenly the hallway seemed to close in on Mel, seemed to be filled with that same heavy tension. Mel's previous arousal sprang back to vivid, clamoring life, and she was sure her knees were shaking. Any minute now and they'd just give out on her.

Her gaze moved slowly over Crys's body. She told herself it was inappropriate, but she couldn't seem to prevent herself from taking in every sensuous, inviting curve.

Crys wore an oversized T-shirt that finished mid thigh, the soft material molding her broad shoulders, caressing the full swell of her naked breasts. Mel's gaze lingered there and took in their rounded fullness, the shadow of Crys's hardened nipples pushing against the cotton.

Mel felt an intense rush of desire. Her nipples contracted, tingled invitingly, and a spiral of throbbing excitement gathered in the pit of her stomach and rushed to center between her legs. And she felt damp and so very ready.

Her heartbeats accelerated wildly and seemed to rise in her chest, thundering like drumbeats in her ears, and she swallowed convulsively. Surely Crys must hear them too.

She looked up and flushed with embarrassment, for she sensed that Crys was aware of her blatant scrutiny. Mel swallowed again, and her tongue tip moistened her dry lips.

"I've been working," she said, her voice sounding decidedly thin. "I couldn't seem to sleep."

"Neither could I," said Crys softly.

CHAPTER ELEVEN

"Must have been the music," Mel offered lamely. "Or something."

"Yes. It must have been."

"Hungry?" Mel asked. Crys put her hand on her throat, her fingers worrying the neckline of her nightshirt. "I could get you a cookie," Mel added in a rush. "Or you could have this half of mine." Mel took a step forward, stopped, and shakily held out the remainder of her cookie.

Crys's gaze went from the cookie to Mel's face, and Mel drew an unsteady breath.

And then slowly Crys was leaning forward, taking a small bite of the cookie Mel clasped. Mel couldn't take her eyes from Crys, watched her, felt as though all of Crys's movements were in slow motion. Crys's dark head coming forward, her soft mouth opening, her white teeth taking hold of the cookie, her lips settling around it, biting off a small piece.

Mel barely caught back a low moan as Crys straightened and looked up at Mel. And she saw a faint question in the shadowy angles of her face.

"You are the most beautiful woman I've ever seen in my life." For a moment Mel couldn't be sure she'd actually said the words or simply thought them. But of course she had said them. The deep huskiness of the comment only vaguely sounded like her voice, but the words reverberated about the hallway, echoed tantalizingly away, and then just as provocatively returned.

Mel watched as Crys swallowed the mouthful of cookie, and she saw her hand move to her throat, as though the food had lodged there and she needed to force it down. Mel swallowed in sympathy, and the air about them grew impossibly more oppressive.

"Mel, I —" Crys stopped, swallowed again.

In the shadowy light, Mel saw the subtle change in her expression. Her dark eyes seemed to glow, and then her eyelids lowered, her thick lashes fanning her cheeks. As Mel watched, Crys's lips trembled slightly, begging to be kissed.

Afterward Mel couldn't have said who made that

153

first move, but they seemed to sway into each other. What remained of the cookie fell from Mel's fingers as her arms slid around Crys's body. As Mel drew Crys against her, she felt the breath she'd been holding hiss between her lips.

The touch of Crys's breasts against Mel seared her, and their impression burned indelibly onto her hot body.

Crys looked up, and her gaze met Mel's and held. Without breaking that eye contact, Mel slowly slid her hands sensuously down the contours of Crys's back, her fingers cupping Crys's buttocks, moving her closer as she strained to merge with her, thigh to thigh, stomach to stomach, her pelvis tilting into Crys.

Mel instinctively moved her hips, and a low, soft moan escaped Crys's mouth, her breath warmly teasing Mel's chin. Mel lowered her head and put her lips to the fullness of Crys's, and suddenly the fire that had been smoldering burst into flame, raged out of control. They clung together, lips tasting, tongues tantalizing, until, gasping for breath, they drew apart.

"Crys," Mel whispered brokenly, and Crys seemed to sag against the wall, needing its support.

Mel followed her, her hands on Crys's body, slowly exploring the outline of her hips, the indentation of her narrow waist, her firm, flat midriff, and finally the heaviness of her breasts.

Crys's nipples were hard peaks thrusting against her nightshirt, and Mel's thumbs found them, grazed them incitingly, and Crys groaned again.

"God, Mel! I can't — I need to touch you, too," she said brokenly, and her fingers fumbled with Mel's sweater, got tangled in her nightshirt.

Mel gave a choked laugh and tore her sweater and

nightshirt off together, tossing them in a heap on the floor.

Slowly Crys reached out, her hands settling gently on Mel's waist as she gazed at Mel's naked breasts. Mel's nipples were erect. They felt so hard she thought they'd explode as she waited for Crys to touch them. When Crys leaned forward, licked first one and then the other with the tip of her tongue, Mel lost whatever control she still had.

Somehow they were in Crys's room, the bedside lamp throwing a shadowy glow over them as Mel shakily pulled Crys's nightshirt over her head. Then she stood transfixed and drank in the sight of Crys's naked body, the absolute beauty of her. Her full, dusky-tipped breasts. Her smooth, rounded hips. Her intriguing triangle of curling dark hair.

She murmured low in her throat as she reverently reached out and let one fingertip lightly trail over Crys's shoulder, over the swell of her left breast, to encircle the engorged nipple. Crys drew a sharp, ragged breath.

Mel's questing finger meandered down the valley between Crys's breasts, dropped lower to dart in and out of Crys's navel, slid over the swell of Crys's stomach, reached the dark, curl-covered mound. She cupped Crys's pubes with the palm of her hand and then let her fingers dip into the musky dampness and slide gently into the delicious folds.

"Mel, I have to . . . I can't stand up," Crys murmured hoarsely, and she sank onto the bed.

Mel went to follow her, but stopped and hurriedly discarded her track pants and socks. She went to move over Crys, but Crys put out her hand.

"No. Stop."

A stab of fear jabbed at Mel. Was Crys going to push her away? Surely not? Mel didn't think she could bear it again.

Crys lay back, resting on one elbow, the fullness of her breasts drawing them sideways. "Wait," she said, her voice thick. "I want . . . I want to look at you, too."

Mel stood before her, the lamplight playing over her, and she felt Crys's heavy-lidded gaze as though Crys had reached out and touched her. She saw herself — her tall body, her breasts that were far more compact than Crys's, her narrow hips and long legs, and she flushed. Would Crys find her slender contours wanting?

"So long and sleek," Crys said thickly. "So beautiful. Just as I imagined you'd be."

Immensely relieved, Mel moved then, stretched out her length beside Crys, delighting in the sensual softness of Crys's skin. She ran her hand over Crys's body again, kissed her sensitive earlobe, slid her tongue tip along the line of Crys's jaw, and rediscovered her sweet, velvety lips.

"Tell me what to do, what you like," Mel whispered brokenly against Crys's mouth.

"There's no hurry. We have plenty of time." Crys gently pushed Mel back onto the bed, and Mel's nerve endings went wild, exalted with a rush of unimaginable yearning.

Crys's hands moved over the planes of Mel's face, her forehead, her eyelids, her straight nose. When they reached Mel's mouth, Mel opened her lips, pursed them around Crys's seeking fingertips.

Then Crys continued her journey, over Mel's chin and throat, settling momentarily, enticingly, on her chest, before Crys's whole hand at last cupped Mel's burgeoning breast. Her fingers teased Mel's nipples, concentrating first on one and then the other, and then Crys leaned forward, replacing her hand and fingers with her mouth and tongue.

Mel moaned softly, feeling her muscles tense as a reckless craving coursed through her. She felt herself building so quickly toward a climax.

While Crys's lips were still on Mel's breast, Mel realized Crys's fingers were sliding sensually downward. When they at last found Mel's clitoris, Mel arched almost immediately, tremors of release taking her by surprise.

"Mmm. So quick," Crys murmured thickly, and Mel could only focus on Crys's fingers still moving so wondrously within her, tantalizing her.

"Please," she heard herself beg, her voice so deeply aroused she barely recognized it. "Don't stop."

Crys had pushed herself up on the bed and trailed her lips down over Mel's hot skin, and Mel's hands cupped Crys's head, her fingers luxuriating in Crys's thick dark hair. Then Mel's entire body seemed to gather itself, climbed impossibly upward, and hovered so awesomely at the peak. Crys's fingers slid in Mel's wetness, and when her lips and tongue found Mel's center, Mel catapulted over the edge, racing downward, gliding on a wave of sensation, before finally coming to a breathtaking rest.

Mel then realized she'd clutched Crys head to her, and she released her hold. Crys slid upward, her face nuzzling against Mel's breast. Mel's legs had flexed, too, holding Crys's fingers in place, and she slowly relaxed her grip.

"I'm sorry. Did I hurt you?" she asked, and Crys kissed her gently.

"Of course not. You were wonderful."

Their eyes met, and Mel felt a glow of love swell in her chest. She changed position and pushed herself up, using a gentle pressure to roll Crys onto her back.

"Let me . . . I want to . . ." Mel swallowed and gave a soft laugh. "I want to return the favor."

A shadow of uncertainty crossed Crys's face. "You don't have to, Mel. I mean . . ."

Mel's fingers grazed Crys's nipples, and Mel heard Crys catch her breath.

"I think I do have to," Mel said hoarsely and lowered her head to suckle on Crys's breast. She gave one full breast her attention and then slid her mouth sideways and paused to delve into the hollow between Crys's breasts before claiming the other, tasting and drawing in the erotic scent of the other woman. As Mel tenderly pulled Crys's nipple into her mouth, Crys groaned.

"God, Mel! That's incredible."

Mel's fingers glided downward, and as they found the dark curls Crys instinctively opened her legs. Mel let her fingers move, took her lead from Crys's responsive nuances.

Crys murmured low in her throat, her muscles tensing rhythmically, and Mel shifted her position, ran her tongue tip down over Crys's stomach, drew in the heady scent of Crys's arousal. Crys made a faint protest, but Mel persisted.

"No. Let me. Please." Then she continued her journey, moving her lips over the wet curls, her tongue finding Crys's center. She matched Crys's movements with her own strokes, with her lips, her tongue, her questing fingers.

Crys cried out as she orgasmed, and Mel moved back to cradle the other woman in her arms.

"I can't tell you how" — Crys gulped a breath — "how fantastic that was."

Mel grinned. "My aim was to please."

Crys looked lazily into Mel's eyes. "You're simply fantastic, do you know that? How could you know . . . ?" Crys shook her head faintly, and Mel shrugged.

"It does take two."

Crys leaned forward and kissed Mel softly, slowly, and then she lay back with a sigh. "It's almost dawn," she said, and Mel looked toward the French doors.

"So it is," she said and pulled Crys into the curve of her arm as she slid her other arm warmly around Crys.

Their legs moved until they were naturally entwined and they relaxed together, slipping into an exhausted sleep.

The sun was well up when Mel woke. She blinked, trying to orient herself. And then she realized she was in Crys's room, in her bed, and her arms were still wrapped around the other woman.

Mel drew in a breath, smelled the warm, so wonderful scent that was Crys, and she sighed contentedly.

This close she could see the fine blue veins crisscrossing the top of Crys's pale breast, the light freckles on the skin of her shoulder, the fine lines radiating from the corners of her eyes. Mel sighed, her breath gently moving the fine strands of Crys's dark hair, and Crys stirred.

Mel ran her tongue tip over the curve of Crys's bare shoulder, and Crys opened her eyes and looked straight into Mel's. Mel felt her draw a sharp breath.

Crys shifted, turned onto her back, and Mel was forced to release her grip on the other woman. Crys continued to stare up at the ceiling.

"Good morning," Mel said lightly and raised her head a little to look at the clock. "Well, it's almost afternoon."

Crys looked at the clock, too, and sat up. The bed-clothes fell away, and Mel's gaze went to Crys's fabulous breasts. Then Mel realized Crys was looking around for her nightshirt. But, of course, that was somewhere on the floor on Mel's side of the bed where Mel had discarded it.

"If you're looking for your nightshirt, it's over here somewhere," Mel said. She was surprised to see a dull flush color the other woman's face. "But you don't have to cover up for me. In fact, I prefer it if you don't." Mel reached out and let her fingers move lightly down Crys's bare arm.

Crys turned away again and ran her hand shakily over her eyes. "Mel, I —" She stopped and shook her head slightly.

"Crys? What's wrong?" Mel pushed herself up onto her elbow so she could see Crys's face.

"Nothing." Crys shrugged. "And everything, I guess."

Mel swallowed. She couldn't seem to find her voice. Was Crys sorry about what had happened?

A heavy silence enveloped them until Crys eventually gave a soft laugh. "Well, now you know," she said lightly.

"Know?" Mel frowned.

"What it's like to sleep with a woman."

"Sleep with . . . ?" Mel slowly digested what Crys had said, what she meant. "You think that's what this was?" she asked carefully. "An experiment? Some sort of carryover from my adolescent yearning?"

"Well, wasn't it?" Crys asked, her voice sounding thick and emotion filled.

Mel swallowed painfully again. "You know it wasn't."

"That's the trouble. At the moment I don't know what to think." Crys took a deep, steadying breath. "At least this time I don't feel quite so guilty. Now I know you're old enough to know what you're doing," she said flatly, and Mel suddenly wanted to cry.

"I told you before, Crys. I knew what I was doing the first time. Oh, I may not have had the moves down pat but, believe me, I knew exactly what I wanted to do."

Crys turned back to face her. "Mel, you were barely seventeen."

"I knew I wanted to kiss a woman. And not just any woman. I wanted to kiss you."

"Mel, you don't —"

"Don't what? Don't know what I'm saying?" Mel gave a short laugh. "Oh, yes, I do. I'm not a naive teenager any more. And I haven't been living in a nunnery, believe me."

Crys's face paled slightly. "Have you . . . ?"

Mel saw Crys swallow, watched the pulse beat erratically at the base of her throat, that wonderful throat, and she felt the ache of desire again as it clutched at the pit of her stomach. Unconsciously her eyes narrowed. "Have I made love to another woman? Yes, I have."

"But —" Crys moved her head uncertainly. "Terry. You'd been together for years."

"Yes, we had." Mel sighed. "I met Terry when I was twenty-one. We became lovers a few months later."

"Then when . . . ?" Crys frowned and Mel grimaced.

"Terry is a woman," she said softly.

CHAPTER TWELVE

Crys was obviously flabbergasted. "Terry is a woman?" she repeated in astonishment.

Mel nodded. "Yes. She is. My partner, Marie-Therese."

"Marie-Therese? My God!" Crys went to continue and then closed her mouth. "Does your mother know?" she asked at last.

Mel gave a short laugh. "No. I'm sure she would have told you if she did, don't you think?"

Crys shook her head. "Why didn't you tell her?"

"I wanted to," Mel said unhappily. "But Terry's, well, paranoid about coming out to families."

"Don't you think that choice was yours when it came to your own family?" Crys asked, and Mel sighed.

"I guess I took the easy way out. In the beginning it was sort of a joke, that Mum had taken it for granted Terry was a male. And then it went on for so long it just got harder to tell her. I knew Mum would be shocked, and part of me didn't want to upset her, or Bill and Amber and Dad. So" — Mel shrugged — "it was easier to let her keep thinking Terry was a guy."

"Oh, Mel."

Mel looked across at Crys. "I know. It's going to be more difficult, more complicated telling Mum now after misleading her for so long. I didn't plan it that way. Honestly."

"I didn't think you would have," Crys acknowledged.

"But I do intend to tell her," Mel continued. "I was going to before I came down here, but you know what Mum's like. She was all fired up packing and organizing Bill, and there just wasn't . . . the time didn't seem right to say, 'Oh, by the way, Mum, I'm a lesbian.' "

Crys absently rubbed her jaw with her hand, and Mel swallowed.

"Did you tell your parents about, well, that you were a lesbian?" she asked, and Crys met her gaze again.

"My father died when I was about five or six. A car accident. After that I think my mother gave up on life. Oh, she didn't exactly throw herself on his funeral pyre, but she never seemed the same after he was killed."

Crys grimaced. "When the headmistress told her about my youthful indiscretion, kissing another girl, she barely reacted. I never told her about Diane because I sensed she didn't want to know. And she died before I met Paul. So I guess I have no right to dictate what you should or shouldn't say to your parents, Mel."

"It's complicated, isn't it?"

Crys nodded. "I guess it is."

"And we've just made it more so," Mel added carefully.

Crys's gaze dropped from Mel's. "It doesn't have to be."

A coldness clutched at Mel's heart. "You mean we can just forget this morning ever happened."

"I didn't exactly mean that," Crys put in.

"Like last time," Mel finished bitterly.

"Mel, that was . . . you know, it wasn't a good time for either of us."

Mel ran her hands through her tousled hair. "I know it wasn't. Things were crazy. We both had our own demons then. You'd just lost David. I was so confused." Mel glanced across at Crys again. "I even slept with Gary after I kissed you."

"Oh, Mel." Crys looked distressed.

"Not because of you." Mel said quickly. "Because of me. I felt weird, not normal. I thought I needed to prove something to myself."

"I didn't mean to make you feel there was something wrong with you, Mel," Crys said earnestly. "Believe me, I know I should have been there for you, been more supportive. I know how frightening it all is when you feel you're different from everyone else, but I, I couldn't cope with what was going on in my own life just then. I had nothing left to give myself. Or you."

"I know that, Crys. Really. And I don't know why I felt the way I did. I mean, I'd grown up with you and you were a lesbian and didn't have two heads or anything. With hindsight, if I hadn't been such a, well, self-centered little prig, I wouldn't have put it on you the way I did. I certainly didn't plan to kiss you that afternoon. It just happened. And later I was horrified I'd done it."

Crys bit her lip. "I didn't realize back then that you and Gary had got so involved. And your mother mustn't have suspected either, or she'd have discussed it with me."

Mel rolled her eyes. "I'll bet she would have." She sighed. "When Gary started to get heavy after the movies the next weekend I thought, why not? How can I reject something I've never tried? I told myself other women had sex with men all the time so there must be something in it." Mel shrugged and smiled crookedly. "Do you suppose that sort of thinking, that kind of female mind-set, is all that perpetuates the species?"

"It might at that," Crys replied with a faint smile at Mel's attempt at a joke.

"Well, there wasn't anything in it for me," Mel added. "Quite honestly, I was totally unimpressed."

"Mel, the first time isn't always the best gauge," Crys began.

"I know. I told myself that too. Physically it was

uncomfortable, and I guess Gary was as inexperienced as I was. But it never got any better for me, Crys. I was relieved when I went down to college in Melbourne, relieved I, well, could stop doing it."

"Is that when you . . . ?" Crys paused.

"Tried a woman?" Mel finished for her, and Crys gave a faint nod. "Not straightaway. I was too, I don't know, too much of a coward, I guess. And I still thought I was a freak. Then I met Terry at a party, and we hit it off right away. She's a bit older than I am and she'd had other girlfriends. I guess you'd say she was experienced."

Mel realized her fingers were worrying at the bedcovers, and she clasped her hands together. "The first time Terry and I made love I knew what had been missing when I did it with Gary. So freak or not, I knew I was a lesbian."

"And you and Terry really did break up over another woman?" Crys asked gently.

Mel nodded. "Oh, yes. I thought Terry and I had a fairly solid, committed relationship. Then she told me she was seeing Maureen and wanted out." Mel shrugged. "That was it."

"I'm sorry."

"I was too. Back then." Mel's words seemed to hover over them.

"And now Terry's not seeing Maureen any more."

"So she tells me."

"How do you feel about that?" Crys asked.

Mel frowned. "Indifferent, I guess you'd say." Mel glanced sideways at Crys, unsure of Crys's reaction to her words. Mel saw the throb of the pulse at the base of Crys's throat, and she felt a tingle of renewed desire. Mel wanted to reach out and mold her hands to Crys's breasts, but something held her back. She had no idea how Crys felt about all this.

Crys moved then, slid from the bed, and Mel's mouth went dry just looking at her naked body.

"I think I need a shower and some coffee," Crys said lightly.

"Crys." Mel swung her legs over the side of the bed.

"Let's take a break, Mel." Crys's words halted Mel. "I need time to, well, digest all this. Can we talk later?"

Mel hesitated and then nodded reluctantly. Crys continued on into her en suite.

Mel pushed herself to her feet, stretched her muscles, and felt the pull of wanting again. She paused, considered joining Crys in her shower, and then turned away. Crys had said she needed time, and Mel had to respect that. She conceded that all this must have been something of a shock for Crys, and Mel was prepared to give her all the time she wanted to get used to it all.

Feeling the strength of resolution, Mel decided there was one thing she was sure of. After those few delightful hours this morning, of having Crys in her arms at long last, she wasn't going to give up on what they had. Not without a fight.

Mel went through to the bathroom and stepped beneath the warm shower spray. She ran her hands over her body and felt her skin tingle as she imagined her own hands were Crys's, gliding over her as they'd done so delightfully just hours ago. And Mel went weak with renewed desire.

She'd waited so long to make love with Crys, and now she suspected she'd never want to stop. She had fallen head over heels in love with Crys, and that wasn't going to change any time soon.

But hadn't she believed she was in love with Terry just six short months ago? The thought came out of nowhere, and Mel paused.

She had loved Terry, but she'd known it was over right from the minute Terry had admitted to breaking their commitment. Terry's betrayal had killed that love. But Mel knew now she'd stubbornly held onto the relationship she'd had with Terry during the long months after their breakup.

Or perhaps she'd simply clung to the idea of being in love out of habit, or maybe out of the fear of being on her own. For whatever reason it hadn't been healthy, and she was just relieved that she'd pulled herself out of it. Coming home, making the complete physical break from Terry, had been the best thing she could have done.

And now there was Crys. Mel was in love with her. Deeply, burningly, and yet *comfortably*, if that was the right word. She wanted Crys physically just as she'd wanted Terry, and yet not in quite the same way.

With Terry, Mel had always been the follower, always felt she'd been on call, waiting to bend any way Terry wanted. Mel sensed Crys would never ask that of her. With Crys it was a two-way thing. And that's the way a relationship should be. At least, the kind of relationship Mel now realized she wanted.

But all that aside, Mel knew she'd always been a little in love with Crys. Mel had been about ten years old when they first met, and Mel had adored Crys, had followed her around. Later that adoration had developed into the major crush that had had such devastating effects. And now, well, Mel wanted to spend the rest of her life with Crys. Working the farm. Talking. Making love.

Mel played the shower spray over her face. She remembered the first time she and Terry had made love. The excitement. The heady sense of being set free from the ill-fitting mores of convention, of expectations. The wonder of realizing as fact what she had always suspected, that she was a lesbian, that she didn't have to play a part dictated by society.

Then she recalled the illicit kiss she and Crys had shared. It had haunted her consistently over the years, even the years she'd shared with Terry.

Often Mel had felt a burning need to telephone Crys, tell her the truth about Terry. But, of course, she never had. If she talked to anyone, she'd told herself, it should be her mother.

Mel turned and flexed the muscles in her shoulders and back as the water flowed over her. And then she stilled.

Suddenly she remembered the times she'd been kissing Terry and Crys's face had floated to the surface of her consciousness. On those occasions she'd had to force Crys's image from her mind. And for days afterward she would feel vaguely disquieted and out of sorts.

Once, not long after Mel had confided in Terry about her youthful indiscretion with Crys, Terry had accused Mel of wallowing in the past. Terry had arrived home late from college and Mel had been in bed, tired after a day of finishing some freelance work she'd taken on.

Terry had woken Mel with kisses and caresses and Mel had protested, gently telling Terry she was tired and wasn't feeling amorous, but Terry had persisted.

For once Mel had remained firm and had turned over, away from Terry's questing hands. Terry had grown angry, accused Mel of having lovers there while she had been out teaching. Mel had laughed tiredly, thinking Terry was joking, but Terry had been serious. She'd flounced off the bed and paced angrily up and down the room.

"How do I know what you do when I'm not here?" she said bitterly. "It's easy to say you've been working."

Mel sat up. "You can check my study, see for yourself what I've been doing."

"I thought Suzy was all over you at that party last weekend," Terry continued, as though Mel hadn't spoken. "Did you two make a date for when I wouldn't be here?"

"No. We didn't," Mel replied irritatedly. "No one's been here, Terry. I told you, I've been working."

Terry swung around. "Or maybe you've been dreaming about that old broad you were lusting after when you were a kid full of raging hormones."

Mel paused slightly, feeling a stab of guilt. The last time she and Terry had made love Mel had had to thrust away thoughts of Crys.

"Aha!" Terry pointed her finger at Mel. "So that *is* it."

"Terry, please —" Mel began.

"Maybe you should invite the old girl down here for a visit. Didn't you say her partner died last year? She'd probably welcome a roll in the hay by now."

"That's disgusting, Terry. You're being ridiculous. And for your information, Crys's partner died over two years ago."

"All the more reason to invite her down. If she's as hot as you seem to think she is, maybe she'd be interested in a threesome and we could all relive your fantasies."

Mel had climbed deliberately out of bed, picked up her pillow, and slept in the spare room. And it had been a while before she'd accepted Terry's apologies that she'd been drunk, had had a couple of glasses of wine on an empty stomach, and didn't know what she was saying.

Sighing, Mel stepped out of the shower, dried off, and pulled on a pair of jeans and a loose knit top. She walked out to the kitchen. Crys turned from the bench and gave Mel a quick smile.

"I've made us some coffee and sandwiches," she said lightly. "Don't know about you, but I'm famished."

Mel shoved her hands into the pockets of her jeans. "A night of sex will do that to you." She grimaced. "Was that bad taste?" She made a face again. "Shall I just sit down and shut up?"

"Might be a good idea," Crys agreed with a laugh. She sat down opposite Mel, and they both began eating. "Did you finish your —" Crys stopped and frowned as the dog began to bark agitatedly.

Moments later a car pulled into the yard. They both stood up and went outside. Crys took hold of

Rags's collar, and they watched as a tall figure with longish dark hair climbed from the car.

Mel caught her breath and glanced across at Crys. She knew by Crys's pale face that she, too, had recognized their visitor. What could Terry be doing here?

CHAPTER THIRTEEN

Crys cleared the blockage in one of the fine-spray nozzles in the watering system and stood back as she switched the water on again. She cast her eyes over the rows of seedlings. Everything seemed to be working perfectly once more.

She sat back against the bench and sighed. She didn't like Terry Johansen, she decided with regret, telling herself her feelings were the result of more than just jealousy because of what Terry had been to Mel. It was far more complicated than that.

And Crys supposed she was a little jealous of the

other woman. But surely that was natural enough. Terry and Mel had been together for six years, and there was every chance Mel would decide she wanted to go back to Terry.

A rush of tears gathered in her eyes, and Crys valiantly blinked them away before they fell. Crying certainly wasn't going to help the situation.

After being on her own for five years, Crys conceded she could barely entertain the thought of being without Mel now. Somehow it was too painful to consider. And if Mel did leave, could Crys really blame her? It would partially be Crys's own fault, she told herself angrily.

This morning, when she woke up to find herself wrapped in Mel's arms, for one wild irrepressible second she'd simply wanted to clutch Mel to her, tell her how much she loved her, how much she wanted and needed her. Not just for the moment, but forever.

Then hard on the heels of that feeling of exhilaration she'd experienced an earth-shattering uncertainty. Thinking Mel was straight, her voice of reason had clamored that she be cautious, that Mel might be testing the waters, just as she'd done all those years ago. So Crys had taken an emotional step back, given Mel a way out by suggesting Mel had indeed used Crys as an experiment.

She knew she had upset Mel, and Crys had been about to apologize when Mel dropped her bombshell about Terry. For long moments Crys hadn't been able to take in the fact that Terry was a woman, nor had she been able to comprehend its ramifications. Not right away.

And then suddenly it had all fallen into place, the inconsistencies that Angela had worried over, Mel's reticence to discuss Terry with her mother, Terry's frequent coincidental absences, and Mel's reluctance to introduce Terry to her family. The truth would answer so many of Angela's questions.

Yet even then Crys had hesitated, hadn't dared to hope that Mel might genuinely care for her, Crys, the way Crys knew she cared for Mel. Fool that she was, she hadn't had the courage to take what Mel might be offering.

So she'd made herself get out of bed, separate them, when all she'd wanted was to pull Mel to her, make love to her again and again. But she'd wanted to give Mel, give them both, a little space to consider the situation rationally, without the confusing and overwhelming color of the physical enticement.

Physical enticement? Crys grimaced. When Mel walked into the kitchen after her shower Crys had known she was way beyond logical and sensible thought when it came to Mel's enticement, physical or otherwise. She should have thrown discretion to the four winds there and then, but still she'd wavered, wanting Mel to be sure of her own feelings, too.

As Crys saw it, there were so many things to consider. Was Mel really over her breakup with Terry? Did Mel want to stay out here in the country or would she get bored, miss the social whirl of the city? Perhaps they could find a compromise. Crys swallowed painfully.

Well, all that might be completely irrelevant now. Now that Terry was here.

When the tall young woman had stepped from the car, Crys had been completely astounded. It had only taken her moments to recognize Terry as the young woman she'd seen on television with Mel last year. And one glance at Mel's wan face had confirmed her suspicion.

As Terry had stridden toward them Crys had had to admire the other woman's confidence, her self-possession. She was as tall as Mel, and her dark hair swung in soft curls down to shoulder length. She wore dark jeans and, beneath an open, short black-leather jacket, a red close-fitting tank top stretched across her breasts, molding their impressive shape.

"Hi, Mel! Bet you're surprised to see me," she said with a wide smile.

Mel seemed to have lost her power of speech, and Terry's grin widened.

"I can see you are." She turned toward Crys, looked quizzically at the dog that sat quiet but watchful at Crys's side. "Not likely to take my leg off, is he?"

"No. I don't think so." Crys made a slight movement with her hand, and Rags relaxed and stretched out on the ground, pink tongue lolling.

"He's a big dog." Terry looked up and smiled again. "I'm Marie-Therese Johansen, by the way, Mel's writing partner. And you must be Crys." Terry held out her hand. "Mel's told me so much about you."

Crys shook Terry's hand, sliding a glance at Mel, and she saw a dull flush color Mel's face. Crys pulled herself together. "Nice to meet you, Terry," she said evenly. "Mel's told me all about you, too."

Terry's dark eyes narrowed, her gaze going to Mel.

"I've told Crys about Marie-Therese and Terry," Mel put in quickly, regaining some of her composure. "She knows about, well, about us."

"I see." Terry shrugged slightly. "We thought it would be best because of our careers, didn't we, love?"

"Something like that," said Mel offhandedly, and Crys suspected from what Mel had told her that Terry was stretching the truth.

Obviously now entirely over her initial surprise, Mel folded her arms and stood with both feet planted firmly apart. "What brings you all the way up here, Terry?" she asked. Crys could glean nothing from her controlled expression.

"I decided to take a break. And I wanted to see you, talk to you." Terry looked pointedly at Crys. "Privately, if I could."

Mel went to speak, but Crys got in first. "Of course," she said levelly. "I have to get to work anyway. Take Terry into the house, Mel. We've not long brewed the coffee so it should still be hot."

"What about, well, your sandwiches?" Mel reminded Crys, seemingly disconcerted.

"That's all right," Crys assured her. "Terry might like them. I'm not really hungry."

Mel went to object, but Terry broke in on her. "We'll see you later then," she said and stepped pointedly between Crys and Mel.

Crys called the dog and headed over to the shed as Mel and Terry went into the house.

No, she did not like Terry Johansen, Crys reiterated to herself. She glanced down at her wristwatch. What should she do? Terry and Mel had been together for over an hour.

What did Terry want? Crys gave a short laugh, and Rags looked up at her from his position guarding the door.

"I know what Terry wants," she said softly to the dog. "She wants Mel."

And what if Mel wanted Terry too? Somehow Crys didn't think Mel did. Not after this morning. Did she? Now that Crys had met Terry, she couldn't see that the other woman was right for Mel. And was she, Crys, so right for Mel? she asked herself ruthlessly. Heavy doubt crept into Crys's mind.

If she looked at the situation honestly, what could the young and vibrant Mel possibly see in the forty-two-year-old, not exactly svelte, old crone that she, Crys, was?

Terry, on the other hand, was closer to Mel's age. She was certainly not unattractive. And she worked so successfully with Mel. Surely it would be easier for Mel to return to Melbourne with Terry. It was no contest that Crys could see.

Yet this morning Mel had said she loved Crys. Unless Mel's declaration was simply the afterglow of great sex. Fantastic sex.

Crys straightened. She knew she loved Mel too. More than she would have thought it was possible to love again.

And then she thought about Diane. Crys sighed. Their life had been more than a little rocky, but they'd had some good times, too.

Crys had loved Diane, would always remember her. But Crys also knew she had to move on, and she had done so before Angela had suggested Mel come down here. Maybe that had been why Crys had been so uneasy about Mel's visit.

Because she'd always known Mel held a special place in her heart. Even Diane had suspected that. One particular episode stuck in Crys's mind.

It had been after an interschool netball competition. Crys had gone with Angela to watch Mel's team play as she often did. Diane's school had also been competing. As Mel played, Crys had introduced Diane to Angela. By the time Mel's game was over, Diane had had to leave to organize her own team so Crys had never got to actually introduce Mel to Diane. But Angela had pointed out her daughter to the other woman.

Later Diane had half jokingly said to Crys, "So that was the infamous Mel Jamieson."

Crys raised her eyebrows. "*Infamous?* Why is Mel infamous?"

Diane shrugged. "Perhaps that wasn't the word I wanted. Maybe I should have said your favorite Mel Jamieson. Because she is, isn't she?"

"I don't know what you mean, Diane." Crys frowned. "Mel's a great kid."

Diane laughed. "She's hardly a kid. Believe me, Crys, they grow up pretty fast these days."

"Mel might look grown up, but she's really quite, well, naive for her age."

Diane made an exclamation of disbelief. "Oh, sure. If you say so. But I bet she has a big old crush on her good old Auntie Crys."

"Diane, that's rubbish." For some reason Crys had felt more than a little defensive.

"Or maybe Auntie Crys has a crush on little Mel?"

Diane ran her finger along the line of Crys's jaw. "Hmm?"

"For heaven's sake, Diane. Mel is Angela's daughter. I've known her since she was ten years old."

"She's not ten years old any more," Diane said and then laughed at Crys's horrified expression. "I'm sorry, sweetie. You're so easy to tease."

"It wasn't funny," Crys said with as much composure as she could muster.

"Don't be such a stick-in-the-mud. I know you like Mel, and I also know you like me." Diane moved up against Crys and ran her hands over Crys's back and buttocks. "Well, more than like me, I hope," she said softly and kissed Crys's lips.

And a small part of Crys worried that she had to feign a response she didn't at that moment feel.

And now? Crys knew the answer to that. Unconsciously she straightened her spine. So what was she doing here cowering in the shed? she asked herself. Was she going to give up the chance of happiness with Mel without putting up even a token resistance?

The bottom line was that the choice was up to Mel, Crys knew that, but at least Crys could go back to the house and let Mel know how much Crys loved her, how much she wanted Mel to stay. And let Mel know there was an alternative to returning to Melbourne with Terry.

Then the decision was Mel's.

Crys gave the watering system another cursory glance and left the shed, her step faltering as she realized Terry's car had gone. She hadn't heard it leave.

Would Mel have simply left without a word? Surely

not. Crys quickened her pace and hurried into the kitchen, only to stop in the doorway. Relief washed over her as Mel's tall figure turned from the table, freshly cut sandwiches in her hands. Crys took hold of the doorjamb, suddenly needing its solid support.

CHAPTER FOURTEEN

Mel watched as Terry's rented car disappeared out of sight. She felt a slight sadness, a regret for what they'd had together, for the closing of a chapter in her life.

Even if Crys did decide she didn't love Mel the way Mel loved her, Mel knew she could never go back. Seeing and talking to Terry had only convinced Mel of that. Having Terry arrive had been the best thing for both of them. It had put everything into perspective and tied off all the ends and drawn the episode to an amicable conclusion. Once Terry thought about it, Mel was sure she'd see that, too.

"But we were great together, babe," Terry had contended when Mel had suggested just that as they sat in the kitchen over a cup of coffee. "How can you just throw that away? I told you I was desperately sorry about Maureen. I'll apologize a thousand times if you want me to."

"I don't want you to do that. I've told you I accept your apology, but" — Mel shrugged — "if you're honest, Terry, you'll admit things weren't terribly good between us before Maureen came on the scene."

Terry was silent for long moments. "Okay. Maybe we did have our problems, but I think we could have worked them out. We still could."

"We don't want the same things any more. Maybe we didn't in the beginning either."

"Like what? Look, Mel," Terry appealed. "In the beginning it was fantastic. You can't say it wasn't."

"I'm not saying that. It was wonderful," Mel said honestly. "You helped me find myself in so many ways. With me. With my work. You gave me confidence to be myself, I guess. I'm grateful for that, and I'll never forget it."

"So why do you want to kiss it all good-bye?" Terry asked testily.

"I've moved on, Terry. And so have you."

"And we can't move on together?" Terry's quip was heavy with sarcasm.

Mel sighed and shook her head. "No. I don't think we can. But I'd like us to remain friends."

Terry sat quietly, absently running her fingertip

around the rim of her coffee mug. She looked up at Mel. "It's the old dame, isn't it?"

Mel paused and then came to a decision. "Yes. It is."

"I can't believe it." Terry gave a disbelieving laugh. "I mean, she's got a great body, I'll grant you that. But she's years older than you are, Mel."

"Fourteen years to be exact," Mel told her.

"Mel, she —"

"I love her, Terry," Mel said evenly, and Terry sighed.

"She must be really something."

"She is."

"So are you two making the commitment you were always so fond of throwing at me?"

Mel hesitated, and Terry raised her eyebrows.

"You mean this isn't a mutual undying love?"

"I don't know, Terry." Mel made a negating movement with her head. "I don't know how Crys feels."

"Then take her to bed and make up her mind," Terry exclaimed exasperatedly, and Mel laughed.

"You never change. And it's not that simple."

"You never change either," Terry replied. "And it's not that complicated. What's the point of wasting time sitting on your hands. You always did have a tendency to procrastinate, Mel."

"I don't intend to procrastinate," Mel stated defensively, and Terry held up her hand in capitulation.

"Okay. So, do you think you two will get together?" she asked.

"I'm hoping so," Mel said softly.

"Will it make any difference if I tell you I think

you're making a mistake?" Terry asked. "Because as I see it, you're just trying to resurrect a childhood fantasy."

"No, it won't make any difference," Mel replied calmly. "And what I feel for Crys is fantastically real."

Terry looked across at Mel, held her gaze, then she drained her coffee mug and stood up. "Well, I guess that's it then." She shoved her hands into the pockets of her coat. "Are we still working together at least?"

"Of course. If you want to." Mel stood up too. "I've finished the illustrations. Come and see what you think."

They went into the study, and Terry carefully scrutinized Mel's work.

"These are fabulous. Tommy's going to love them. What say I take them back with me?" She grimaced. "Then this won't be a completely wasted trip."

Mel had been going to add a few finishing touches to a couple of the illustrations, but they decided they were fine as they were. Terry helped Mel pack them up, and they carefully stowed them in Terry's car.

"Sure you won't change your mind and come with me, babe?" Terry asked when they'd finished.

Mel shook her head. "No. I kind of like it here."

Terry shook her head. "Bit too back of beyond for me. But if things don't work out, you know where to find me."

"I'm hoping they will work out."

Terry leaned over and kissed Mel on the cheek. "Keep in touch. Okay?"

"Sure. Bye, Terry."

And Terry climbed into the car and drove away.

Mel looked toward the shed and then returned to the house. Terry's arrival had interrupted their brunch so Crys must be starving. She'd just finished making fresh sandwiches when she turned to find Crys standing in the kitchen doorway.

"I was bringing you these," Mel said a little breathily. "I thought you'd be fading away with hunger by now."

Crys seemed to hold herself tensely. "Where's Terry?" she asked, her voice sounding a little thin to her ears.

Mel shrugged. "She's gone."

The air in the kitchen seemed to thicken as the silence stretched between them.

"And I'm staying," Mel added at last. "If you'll have me, that is."

"Of course." Crys swallowed. "You can stay as long as you want."

"I thought perhaps, well —" Mel paused, gathered her courage. "I thought forever," she said. Her heartbeats echoed inside her, and she had trouble catching her breath as she waited for Crys's response.

Crys stayed standing by the door, her hand holding onto the doorjamb. "Are you sure that's what you want?"

Mel shrugged again. "You know what I want, Crys. You've known since I was seventeen years old. I'm just a little unsure about what, about how you feel." Mel watched Crys warily. "I love you, Crys. Deep down I think I always have."

Crys's tensed shoulders suddenly seemed to sag. "Oh, Mel. I love you, too. But I thought . . . you and Terry . . . And there are so many reasons, substantial, logical reasons why we shouldn't even be having this conversation."

Mel carefully put the sandwiches back on the table and walked slowly across until she was standing in front of Crys, almost touching her.

"None of them matter in the least," she said and reached out, pulling Crys into her arms and kissing her.

Crys hesitated for barely a moment before she returned Mel's feverish kiss with a matching hunger.

Mel's hands roved over Crys's body, making Crys moan softly. Her knee insinuated itself between Crys's legs, the pressure of it making Crys cling to Mel, and Mel felt a wild craving grow inside her. And then her hands were reaching under Crys's shirt, pushing it from Crys's shoulders. She unclipped Crys's bra, letting it fall to the floor.

Murmuring her satisfaction, Mel gazed for long moments at Crys's bare breasts, and then she slowly ran her tongue over Crys's skin, taking one hard nipple into her mouth.

Crys trembled, sure her legs would give way beneath her, but Mel held her, supported her against the wall. When eventually Mel drew back, Crys had all but lost control.

"The door." She got out. "What if someone —"

"Comes?" Mel raised her eyebrows. "Besides us, you mean?" she said, and Crys felt her face grow hot.

Mel laughed softly, scooped up Crys's shirt, and gently closed the door. "There. Circumspection reigns again." She took Crys's hand and led her back along the hallway. "If anyone knocks or the phone rings, we'll ignore it."

She kissed Crys again and slowly drew down the

zipper on Crys's jeans and dragged the jeans over her hips until Crys could step out of them. Mel then pulled off her own shirt and jeans and sank onto the bed.

Crys followed her, kneeling over Mel, one leg on either side of Mel's hips, as she settled on Mel's lap. Mel wrapped her arms around Crys and buried her face between Crys's breasts, murmuring ecstatically.

"I love everything about you. The way you feel. The way you smell. The taste of your skin." She ran her tongue across Crys's chest and delighted in feeling Crys tremble in her arms.

Crys threw back her head, and Mel nibbled her way up over Crys's throat and found her lips again. Mel's right hand left Crys's hip, slid down, and paused tantalizingly before slowly seeking, and her fingers then finding, Crys's center. Delighting in Crys's dampness, Mel's fingers gently stroked and circled, making Crys whimper with pleasure. And then Crys cried Mel's name, collapsing against her.

They stretched out side by side then, their hands on each other, fingers touching, seeking out each erotic place. They kissed each other deeply, murmured their love for each other, climbed the heady heights, and claimed the ecstatic release, breathlessly clinging to each other.

"Oh, God! Mel, just hold me," Crys said brokenly, clutching Mel to her as though she'd never let her go.

Mel could feel the dampness of Crys's tears on her hot skin. "Crys? What is it?" she asked worriedly. "Was it that bad?"

"Bad? Oh, no. It was wonderful. I just — After this morning I just didn't think anything could be as good."

Mel relaxed with relief, and she grinned. "Ah. So it was good for you, too?"

"More than good."

Mel sobered. "It was for me, too." She tenderly kissed Crys's soft lips. "You know, I think inside us all we have this small part, the very essence of us, and in it there's a void waiting to be filled. Sometimes we put someone there who doesn't really fit, and that leaves us still felling vaguely empty.

"But when you find that someone who does perfectly fit that special space, well, it's just incredibly right. You" — Mel swallowed — "you're incredibly right for me, Crys, and a part of me has been waiting for you all my life."

Crys looked into Mel's eyes, and her tears welled again. "Mel." She shook her head. "I'm far too old for you. I've hardly had an unblemished past. I'm —"

"The past is past. You're beautiful. You're intelligent. We fit," Mel said simply. "And if I'm right for you, too, then that's the most incredible thing that could happen. We settle into each other." Mel kissed Crys reverently. "Can't you feel that, too?"

"Mel, this is madness. What will people think? Your mother, for one."

Mel grinned crookedly. "We could tell Mum we're just good friends? Or maybe I could just say I have a new boyfriend and that his name is Chris?"

"Mel, please. This is serious."

"I know. And when it comes to how I feel about you, well, I've never been more serious in my life."

"Maybe I'm just some sort of mother figure for you."

"I already have a mother. And whatever her faults, however much she sometimes irritates the hell out of me, she's always been there for me in her own way. You know that."

Crys nodded. "She's always been there for me, too."

"So let's erase the mother figure thing out of the equation."

"That still leaves the fact that there are fourteen years between us."

"Easily fixed. I'll count two years for every one from now on and you can wait at forty-two for me until I catch you. Come on, Crys. Do those fourteen years matter when we're out working together?"

Crys shook her head.

"When we're cleaning or cooking or sitting talking?"

"No."

Mel lowered her voice. "And do they matter when we're here, in bed together, making love?"

The look in Crys's eyes said no.

"I love you, Crys," Mel said. "As I said before, I think I always have. But I had to wait to grow up. And you had commitments to Diane. Before, when I kissed you all those years ago, it wasn't our time. We've both had to wait for that. And now it's here. Let's not pass it up."

Crys buried her face in the curve of Mel's throat. "I wish I didn't feel I was taking advantage of you."

Mel gave an exclamation of disgust. "No one's taking advantage of anyone." She broke off as the ringing of the telephone made them both jump.

Crys automatically picked up the bedside extension. "Crys speaking." She swallowed and sat up. "Angela. How" — she grimaced expressively at Mel — "how are you? Oh. Right. Well, Mel's right here. She's just come in." A dull flush washed Crys's face as she handed Mel the receiver as though it were a hot coal.

Mel raised her eyebrows inquiringly at Crys, who simply shrugged in reply. "Mum? Where are you?" Mel asked, loosening her grip on the phone when she realized her knuckles were turning white.

"I'm at Amber's and Adam's," replied her mother. "Your stepfather's managing all right so, since he forgot some papers he just has to have, I thought I'd come home, collect the relevant papers, and check to see how my girls are getting on."

"Well, that's nice. And I don't know about Amber, but I'm absolutely fine." Mel let her gaze linger suggestively on Crys's naked body and Crys gave her a shove. "Um, are you coming down here?" Mel asked as evenly as she could.

"That's what I was ringing about, and I would have talked to Crys about it if she hadn't handed the phone to you so quickly. I thought I'd drive down tomorrow. Amber's lending me her car for a few days."

Mel swallowed. Her mother was coming down so soon! "That's great, Mum." She took another gulp of air. "Actually, Mum, I have something to tell you. That is, Crys and I" — Mel glanced at Crys again, and Crys rolled her eyes eloquently — "Crys and I have something to tell you."

"Oh, I think I know what that is," said her mother easily.

"You do? Oh, I don't —"

"Yes," continued her mother. "You told Amber you were really enjoying being down there on the farm, so I thought maybe you'd decide to stay on with Crys for a while, take on the job helping her out. Am I right?"

"Mum, you're uncanny." Mel stifled a hysterical giggle. "I love it down here and I am staying. And —"

"I knew it," Angela exclaimed. "When I thought of Crys, I knew the farm would be just the place for you. Who said I don't know my own girls?"

Mel did laugh then. "Oh, I think I can still come up with a surprise or two, Mum."

"Well, I love surprises. You can tell me all about it when I get down there tomorrow. I'm looking forward to seeing you both. Now, Amber and I are taking the children to the park, so I'd better go. Bye, love. And say good-bye to Crys for me."

Mel handed the receiver back to Crys, and she replaced it on its cradle.

"Well, if we had a video phone we wouldn't have to tell Mum anything." Mel gave a half laugh and sighed loudly.

"When is she coming down?" Crys asked resignedly.

"Tomorrow."

Crys groaned. "I don't know if I'm ready for this. Maybe we could just tell her you like it here, that we've become good friends, and then, when she's used to that, we can tell her everything else next time she comes down."

"What everything else are we talking about specifically?" Mel asked softly as she ran her hand over Crys's bare breasts.

Crys caught Mel's wandering fingers and held them firmly in her own. "You know what I mean," she said and kissed the palm of Mel's hand.

"You mean how my hands on your breasts drive you crazy? How my fingers and tongue can —"

"Mel. Stop! Please be serious." Crys frowned, and Mel leaned forward, kissing Crys gently.

"I know it's serious, my darling Crys. So serious I'm not going to settle for anything less than the truth. I'm not going to play any more games of let's pretend. I love you, and I'm going to tell Mum just that."

Crys looked into Mel's eyes. "I don't want to lose your mother's friendship. What if she —"

Mel shook her head. "She won't. It might take her a while to get used to the idea, but she'll come around. I know she will. She loves us both."

"That doesn't always mean that when push comes to shove, things will all fall happily-ever-after into place," Crys warned.

"I know. But for years Mum has supported you, championed the gay and lesbian cause on your behalf. Why would she stop now?"

"Yes, I know. But you're her daughter, Mel. She might see that differently."

"And she might not. She's also brought Amber and me up to believe everyone has a right to free expression." Mel grinned. "At least she's fond of telling us that. Now will come the test, whether she's prepared to stand by her convictions. I'm pretty sure she will. But either way, I'm not going to lose you, what we have." Mel paused and then met Crys's gaze. "What about you?"

"I don't want to lose you, either, Mel. I died a thousand deaths over there in the shed, knowing you were with Terry, that you might leave." Crys took hold of Mel's hand again. "I don't know if you remember, but after you kissed me that first time, you asked me if I loved Diane? And I said I did."

Mel nodded. "I remember."

"I went home and did some thinking in the light of the fact that I'd kissed you back. I knew I did love Diane, but part of me loved you, too. I was horrified at myself. You were so young and I, well, I was tempted, Mel."

Mel grinned broadly. "You were? Really?"

"Oh, yes. Really." Crys shook her head. "You don't know how tempted I was. But I also felt I was committed to Diane. Our lives were bound together, the divorce, the court case. My life was such a mess. I couldn't . . . Diane and I, we had too much history.

"But that was then, Mel. I want to make a new beginning. With you. And I know you're right about telling your mother. Even though I'm worried about how she'll take it, I also think we do owe her the truth." Crys shook her head. "I guess what I'm trying to say is, I love you, Mel."

Mel's smile widened. "And I'm so very glad you do."

Crys laughed a little disconcertedly. "I love you more than I hoped I'd ever love anyone again."

"More than being too terrified to tell my mother you do?" Mel asked, a teasing light making her eyes glow.

"I'm afraid so," Crys said with mock solemnity. "More than life itself."

Mel leaned forward, kissed Crys slowly. "Then this is a two-way thing. We both fit, Crys. That's all that matters, don't you think?" she said softly, drawing Crys into the circle of her arms.

LOOKING FOR NAIAD?

Buy our books at
www.naiadpress.com

or call our toll-free number
1-800-533-1973

or by fax (24 hours a day)
1-850-539-9731

A few of the publications of
THE NAIAD PRESS, INC.
P.O. Box 10543   Tallahassee, Florida 32302
Phone (850) 539-5965
Toll-Free Order Number: 1-800-533-1973
Web Site: WWW.NAIADPRESS.COM
Mail orders welcome. Please include 15% postage.
Write or call for our free catalog which also features an
incredible selection of lesbian videos.

THE TOUCH OF YOUR HAND edited by Barbara Grier and
Christine Cassidy. 304 pp. Erotic love stories by Naiad Press
authors.   ISBN 1-56280-220-8   14.95

WINDROW GARDEN by Janet McClellan. 192 pp. They discover
a passion they never dreamed possible.   ISBN 1-56280-216-X   11.95

PAST DUE by Claire McNab. 224 pp. 10th Carol Ashton
mystery.   ISBN 1-56280-217-8   11.95

CHRISTABEL by Laura Adams. 224 pp. Two captive hearts and
the passion that will set them free.   ISBN 1-56280-214-3   11.95

PRIVATE PASSIONS by Laura DeHart Young. 192 pp. An
unforgettable new portrait of lesbian love . . . ISBN 1-56280-215-1   11.95

BAD MOON RISING by Barbara Johnson. 208 pp. 2nd Colleen
Fitzgerald mystery.   ISBN 1-56280-211-9   11.95

RIVER QUAY by Janet McClellan. 208 pp. 3rd Tru North
mystery.   ISBN 1-56280-212-7   11.95

ENDLESS LOVE by Lisa Shapiro. 272 pp. To believe, once
again, that love can be forever.   ISBN 1-56280-213-5   11.95

FALLEN FROM GRACE by Pat Welch. 256 pp. 6th Helen Black
mystery.   ISBN 1-56280-209-7   11.95

THE NAKED EYE by Catherine Ennis. 208 pp. Her lover in the
camera's eye . . .   ISBN 1-56280-210-0   11.95

OVER THE LINE by Tracey Richardson. 176 pp. 2nd Stevie
Houston mystery.   ISBN 1-56280-202-X   11.95

JULIA'S SONG by Ann O'Leary. 208 pp. Strangely
disturbing . . . strangely exciting.   ISBN 1-56280-197-X   11.95

LOVE IN THE BALANCE by Marianne K. Martin. 256 pp.
Weighing the costs of love . . .   ISBN 1-56280-199-6   11.95

PIECE OF MY HEART by Julia Watts. 208 pp. All the
stuff that dreams are made of —   ISBN 1-56280-206-2   11.95

MAKING UP FOR LOST TIME by Karin Kallmaker. 240 pp.
Nobody does it better . . .   ISBN 1-56280-196-1   11.95

GOLD FEVER by Lyn Denison. 224 pp. By author of Dream
Lover.   ISBN 1-56280-201-1   11.95

WHEN THE DEAD SPEAK by Therese Szymanski. 224 pp. 2nd
Brett Higgins mystery.   ISBN 1-56280-198-8   11.95

FOURTH DOWN by Kate Calloway. 240 pp. 4th Cassidy James
mystery.   ISBN 1-56280-205-4   11.95

A MOMENT'S INDISCRETION by Peggy J. Herring. 176 pp.
There's a fine line between love and lust . . . ISBN 1-56280-194-5   11.95

CITY LIGHTS/COUNTRY CANDLES by Penny Hayes. 208 pp.
About the women she has known . . .   ISBN 1-56280-195-3   11.95

POSSESSIONS by Kaye Davis. 240 pp. 2nd Maris Middleton
mystery.   ISBN 1-56280-192-9   11.95

A QUESTION OF LOVE by Saxon Bennett. 208 pp. Every
woman is granted one great love.   ISBN 1-56280-205-4   11.95

RHYTHM TIDE by Frankie J. Jones. 160 pp.   . . . to desire
passionately and be passionately desired.   ISBN 1-56280-189-9   11.95

PENN VALLEY PHOENIX by Janet McClellan. 208 pp. 2nd
Tru North Mystery.   ISBN 1-56280-200-3   11.95

BY RESERVATION ONLY by Jackie Calhoun. 240 pp. A
chance for true happiness.   ISBN 1-56280-191-0   11.95

OLD BLACK MAGIC by Jaye Maiman. 272 pp. 9th Robin
Miller mystery.   ISBN 1-56280-175-9   11.95

LEGACY OF LOVE by Marianne K. Martin. 240 pp. Women
will do anything for her . . .   ISBN 1-56280-184-8   11.95

LETTING GO by Ann O'Leary. 160 pp. Laura, at 39, in love
with 23-year-old Kate.   ISBN 1-56280-183-X   11.95

LADY BE GOOD edited by Barbara Grier and Christine Cassidy.
288 pp. Erotic stories by Naiad Press authors. ISBN 1-56280-180-5   14.95

CHAIN LETTER by Claire McNab. 288 pp. 9th Carol Ashton
mystery.   ISBN 1-56280-181-3   11.95

NIGHT VISION by Laura Adams. 256 pp. Erotic fantasy romance
by "famous" author.   ISBN 1-56280-182-1   11.95

SEA TO SHINING SEA by Lisa Shapiro. 256 pp. Unable to resist
the raging passion . . .   ISBN 1-56280-177-5   11.95

THIRD DEGREE by Kate Calloway. 224 pp. 3rd Cassidy James
mystery.   ISBN 1-56280-185-6   11.95

WHEN THE DANCING STOPS by Therese Szymanski. 272 pp.
1st Brett Higgins mystery.   ISBN 1-56280-186-4   11.95

PHASES OF THE MOON by Julia Watts. 192 pp. . . . . hungry
for everything life has to offer.   ISBN 1-56280-176-7   11.95

BABY IT'S COLD by Jaye Maiman. 256 pp. 5th Robin Miller
mystery.   ISBN 1-56280-156-2   10.95

CLASS REUNION by Linda Hill. 176 pp. The girl from her
past . . .   ISBN 1-56280-178-3   11.95

DREAM LOVER by Lyn Denison. 224 pp. A soft, sensuous,
romantic fantasy.   ISBN 1-56280-173-1   11.95

FORTY LOVE by Diana Simmonds. 288 pp. Joyous, heart-
warming romance.   ISBN 1-56280-171-6   11.95

IN THE MOOD by Robbi Sommers. 160 pp. The queen of
erotic tension!   ISBN 1-56280-172-4   11.95

SWIMMING CAT COVE by Lauren Douglas. 192 pp. 2nd
Allison O'Neil Mystery.   ISBN 1-56280-168-6   11.95

THE LOVING LESBIAN by Claire McNab and Sharon Gedan.
240 pp. Explore the experiences that make lesbian love unique.
ISBN 1-56280-169-4   14.95

COURTED by Celia Cohen. 160 pp. Sparkling romantic
encounter.   ISBN 1-56280-166-X   11.95

SEASONS OF THE HEART by Jackie Calhoun. 240 pp. Romance
through the years.   ISBN 1-56280-167-8   11.95

K. C. BOMBER by Janet McClellan. 208 pp. 1st Tru North
mystery.   ISBN 1-56280-157-0   11.95

LAST RITES by Tracey Richardson. 192 pp. 1st Stevie Houston
mystery.   ISBN 1-56280-164-3   11.95

EMBRACE IN MOTION by Karin Kallmaker. 256 pp. A whirlwind
love affair.   ISBN 1-56280-165-1   11.95

HOT CHECK by Peggy J. Herring. 192 pp. Will workaholic Alice
fall for guitarist Ricky?   ISBN 1-56280-163-5   11.95

OLD TIES by Saxon Bennett. 176 pp. Can Cleo surrender to a
passionate new love?   ISBN 1-56280-159-7   11.95

LOVE ON THE LINE by Laura DeHart Young. 176 pp. Will Stef
win Kay's heart?   ISBN 1-56280-162-7   11.95

DEVIL'S LEG CROSSING by Kaye Davis. 192 pp. 1st Maris
Middleton mystery.   ISBN 1-56280-158-9   11.95

COSTA BRAVA by Marta Balletbo Coll. 144 pp. Read the book,
see the movie!   ISBN 1-56280-153-8   11.95

MEETING MAGDALENE & OTHER STORIES by
Marilyn Freeman. 144 pp. Read the book, see the movie!
ISBN 1-56280-170-8   11.95

SECOND FIDDLE by Kate 208 pp. 2nd P.I. Cassidy James
mystery.   ISBN 1-56280-169-6   11.95

LAUREL by Isabel Miller. 128 pp. By the author of the beloved
Patience and Sarah.   ISBN 1-56280-146-5   10.95

LOVE OR MONEY by Jackie Calhoun. 240 pp. The romance of
real life.   ISBN 1-56280-147-3   10.95

SMOKE AND MIRRORS by Pat Welch. 224 pp. 5th Helen Black
Mystery.   ISBN 1-56280-143-0   10.95

These are just a few of the many Naiad Press titles — we are the oldest and
largest lesbian/feminist publishing company in the world. We also offer an
enormous selection of lesbian video products. Please request a complete
catalog. We offer personal service; we encourage and welcome direct mail
orders from individuals who have limited access to bookstores carrying our
publications.